Edie
and
the
Flits
in
PARIS

First published in Great Britain in 2022 by
PICCADILLY PRESS
4th Floor, Victoria House
Bloomsbury Square
London WC1B 4DA
Owned by Bonnier Books
Sveavägen 56, Stockholm, Sweden
www.piccadillypress.co.uk

A CIP catalogue record for this book is available from the British Library.

ISBN: 978-1-80078-158-0

Also available as an ebook and in audio

1

Typeset by Envy Design Ltd
Printed and bound in Great Britain by Clays Ltd, Elcograf S.p.A.

Piccadilly Press is an imprint of Bonnier Books UK
www.bonnierbooks.co.uk

Edie
and
the
Flits
in
PARIS

KATE WILKINSON

illustrated by Joe Berger

Piccadilly
PRESS

For my extended family in Sweden and the Netherlands – forever European.

Mind the Gap

Shadwell rested for a moment in the branches of a plum tree. He shook out his wings and hooked the eyeglass he was carrying onto a convenient twig. He wasn't stopping here for long; he had a delivery to make. Shadwell had barely given a thought to the old owner of the eyeglass since he flew out of the London Underground tunnel at Bow Road. He wasn't a loyal bird and he knew which side his wings were feathered.

He hopped down onto a bird table and gave a loud, raspy crow call that caused the smaller birds to scatter. *Kraaa!*

He hoovered up some mealworms and cocked his head to one side to check that the precious eyeglass was still there. The wind ruffled his feathers and the air had a salty tang to it. From where he was perched, he could just see a rectangle of blustery sky and the distant line of the sea.

Time to go.

Shadwell plucked the eyeglass from the tree and headed east, bracing himself for the crossing.

Chapter One

Highgate Station

Edie Winter glanced behind her as she heard the crack of a stick. A small, hooded figure was pushing their way through the raggedy line of hedging.

Edie bristled and looked at Naz. They had already made their way through the clumps of autumn bramble and were standing on the deserted station platform that lay over Highgate Underground. Only she, Naz and Charlie knew about this place. Or so she thought. It was almost a year since Edie and her friends had rescued the flits from Vera Creech, and yet she still felt uneasy whenever she visited the Hillside Camp.

The hedge rustled and shook. Whoever it was seemed to have caught their coat on a thorn and was tugging at it.

'Charlie, is that you?' Edie called out. She could already see that the imposter looked much too small to be Charlie, and he wasn't supposed to be here for another half an hour.

The figure emerged with her hood pushed back off her head and a fan of twigs caught in her hair.

'Sami!' said Naz. 'What are you *doing* here?'

'I wanted to know where you go every week,' said Sami, picking her way through the brambles towards them. 'So I followed you.'

'But Mum will be home by now and wondering where you are. You shouldn't have done that!' Naz said crossly. 'And you've torn your coat.'

Naz's younger sister didn't look sorry at all. If anything, she looked triumphant.

'I left a note,' she said lightly. 'I wrote, *Naz and Edie have taken me on an adventure! Back later.*'

A loud ping on Naz's phone told her that Mrs Balik had just found the note and had questions. Naz moved away from Edie to call her and Edie could hear snatches of the conversation.

'Yes, Mum, it's fine. She's with me.'

Edie felt a hot flush of annoyance. Sami was always following them around, banging on Naz's door, rooting through their bags or hiding under Naz's bed. She suspected that Sami had been eavesdropping behind the sofa when they talked about the flits, and she had spotted Sami watching them from the front-room window as they left each week to walk over here from Alexandra Palace.

'Is this the place where they live?' Sami asked.

'Where who lives?' said Edie flatly.

'The things you keep talking about. The flits.'

'It might be,' said Edie. She decided that being vague was the best tactic for now.

'Are they like fairies?'

'NO!' said Edie. 'They're *not* fairies.'

'What are they then?' The other thing about Sami was that she asked endless questions.

'They're like . . . small people.'

'People?'

Naz finished talking to Mrs Balik and joined them again. She shrugged her shoulders at Edie and mouthed 'sorry' while Sami continued with her list of questions.

'Are they made of plastic . . . like LEGO people?'

Edie and Naz looked at each other, both wondering if answering 'yes' might curb Sami's curiosity, but it seemed wrong to turn something as real and alive as the flits into stiff figures made of plastic. Edie felt the familiar whir of gossamer wings and another voice joined the fray.

'What's taking you so long?'

A flit hovered in front of her nose, so close that Edie almost had to cross her eyes to see her. She held up her hand and Impy settled on the pad of her thumb.

'And who's that?' Impy said, pointing at Sami.

For once, Sami was completely silent. She lifted herself up onto the balls of her feet, almost not daring to blink as she stared at Impy.

Edie realised that she could no longer pretend.

'Look, Sami, you mustn't tell anyone else,' she said.

Sami nodded furiously and Edie lowered her hand so that it was level with Sami's face.

'Impy, I want you to meet Sami. Sami is Naz's little sister.'

Sami gave a tiny suck of air and her mouth froze half open. Then she held out a wobbly hand and Impy obligingly hopped onto it and adjusted her sweet-wrapper clothes.

'You really are alive!' Sami croaked in a half-whisper.

'I should hope so,' said Impy. She scowled a little at Sami. 'How old are you?'

'I'm eight,' said Sami. 'And a half.'

Impy beamed at this and tugged at Sami's finger. 'Shall I show you round?'

Sami managed to croak out a 'yes, please!'

'Don't be scared,' said Edie.

'I'm not,' said Sami firmly, and together they jumped down onto the old tracks and moved towards the bank where the flits had their camp.

Edie still felt annoyed with Sami, but it was hard to remain angry when she could see Sami's wide-eyed astonishment. She couldn't help but think back to how *she* had felt the same fizz of excitement when she had first discovered the flits inside an abandoned box on the London Underground. As Impy led them closer to the bank, Edie also remembered how she had come here with Impy and Nid and discovered their camp broken and deserted.

They stood in a row in front of the jaunty line of flit houses, now fully repaired with recycled rubbish and items foraged from the Underground. Some were crafted out of tin cans and jam jars, and others were built from lollipop-stick planking and cereal-packet walls. A crisp bag lined a roof to stop the rain coming in, a drinking straw acted as a gutter and washing hung from a piece of string and two paper clips. She felt a tiny pang of jealousy as Impy showed Sami the camp for the first time.

'The flits are foragers,' she said, following behind as if she was a teacher guiding a school trip. 'They find everything they need left behind by humans on the Underground. And they're really *not* fairies, Sami.' But Sami didn't need to be told. She stared at everything, carefully taking in every detail. She paused as her eyes drew level with a tunnel slide made from a piece of old hose pipe and she stood entranced by the younger flits, who were taking it in turns to slide through it.

'Ohhhh!' she breathed.

'This way,' said Impy, leading her further along the street by the finger to Number 9. Impy drew back a square of canvas and there they all were. Jot and Speckle washing up, Flum seated on a cork reading and Nid juggling his beads. Standing in an anchovy tin filled with water was Pea, the newest member of Impy's family.

Sami, still open-mouthed, stared at the small tin bath that Pea stood in wearing a pair of tin-foil boots, and Pea's tiny eyes grew round as she stared back at Sami's giant human face filling the canvas doorway.

'Who's that?' Sami asked Impy.

'Oh, that's just my little sister, Pea,' said Impy dismissively. 'Shall I show you my –'

But Sami couldn't take her eyes off Pea. She dipped her little finger in the anchovy tin and gently flicked a drop of water at Pea. At first Pea drew back, but when Sami did it again, she clapped her hands and, screeching with laughter, splashed Sami back.

'I felt just the same when you showed me this camp last year,' Naz whispered. 'I thought it was the most magical thing I'd ever seen. And now look at Sami!'

Edie nodded, but she felt strangely conflicted. She felt like she was giving something away and she wasn't quite ready.

Chapter Two

The Hillside Camp

Charlie was waiting in the car park near the entrance to the station. He waved as Edie pushed her way back through the hedge but then carried on looking at something on his phone. He was dressed in his usual uniform for Scouts, but he had grown almost a foot since Edie had first met him and his trousers were now dangling above his ankles.

'All right?' he said as she drew alongside him.

'I've got you a birthday present,' she said and hooked her arm through his. Charlie's thirteenth birthday was in two days' time. He smiled, but she could feel his shoulders stiffen a little.

They pushed back through the hedge and jumped down onto the tracks at the end of the deserted platform. Naz and Sami turned and waved at them from the flit camp and Charlie paused. Edie wondered if he was cross that Sami was here, so she tried to explain what had happened.

'It's fine, Edie,' said Charlie, but he stayed standing just in front of the platform. Then he said a very strange thing. 'Is this the right place?'

Edie stared at him, wondering if he was joking, but he looked deadly serious.

'Of course it is!' she said. 'Charlie, you've been here a hundred times.'

Charlie nodded but he looked strangely blank.

'Come and see what Nid's doing!' Sami called out to them.

Edie dragged Charlie towards the camp. She introduced Sami properly and he nodded awkwardly at her and Naz but didn't say anything.

Edie watched Nid for a while as he slid on his front down the hose-pipe slide and did a series of star jumps to impress his new audience. Sami whooped and clapped as if it was the best show she'd ever seen, but Edie became aware that Charlie had drifted away again. He was sitting behind them on the edge of the platform, swinging his legs and fiddling with his phone. She left Naz and Sami and walked back to stand in front of him, crossing her arms.

'What are you doing sitting back here?'

'Nothing much,' Charlie said, without looking up.

Edie tried again. 'Benedict says hello and Dad's still getting fan mail from other lost property offices.'

'Is he. Why?'

'Because of what happened last year, Charlie!' Edie was beginning to feel irritated. 'At Wilde Street ghost station?'

'Oh, yeah. Of course.'

To fill the increasingly awkward gaps, Edie pulled a package out of her coat pocket.

'Happy Birthday for Saturday,' she said. 'Dad helped me choose it. I can't believe you're going to be thirteen.'

'Thanks, Edie,' he said, flashing her a quick smile. He opened the package and inside was a book – *The Big Book of Knots*.

'Oh, that's brilliant!' he said, and for the first time that day he showed genuine interest.

Edie glanced over at Sami and Naz and the flit camp. 'Do you remember how we felt when we first met the flits?'

She thought back to how much she cared about them and would do anything to help them, and the relief when she found Charlie and discovered that he did too. She turned back to Charlie, but he was flicking through the pages of the knot book.

'Charlie?' Edie said. 'Did you even hear what I said?'

She pointed towards the camp and he looked up
– but he seemed bewildered, as if he was struggling to
grasp what they were doing there. Then he glanced at
his watch. Edie almost couldn't bring herself to think it.
Charlie looked a tiny bit . . . *bored*!

'What is the matter with you?' Edie exploded.

Charlie looked uncomfortable. 'Edie, I . . .' Then an
indescribable sadness washed over his face, as if he knew
that he was losing something but he didn't quite know
what it was.

'I should really get going,' he said.

Edie pressed her hands to her hot cheeks. She felt furious with Charlie. How could he, after all they had been through together, be so NORMAL? Impy had told them, soon after they had met, that 'normal' children couldn't see them any more once they became teenagers, but she and Charlie were special. Weren't they? She didn't think *they* would stop seeing the flits just because they were thirteen!

'Aren't you going to say goodbye to Impy and Nid?'

'Oh, er . . . bye!' Charlie said to no one in particular. 'And thanks again, Edie, for the present!'

Impy *was* right. Charlie's thirteenth birthday was only two days away and already he was forgetting about the flits. As she watched Charlie go, she felt something sliding away from her, like sand down a chute. Would they ever meet here again?

Impy appeared alongside her, whirring past her ear and settling herself on Edie's shoulder.

'Charlie's gone,' said Edie in a small voice.

'It's always the same. They never say goodbye properly,' Impy said.

'But he and Nid were such good friends!' said Edie.

'We get used to it.'

'Did you know he was going to be thirteen this week?' said Edie.

'Of course,' said Impy. 'We always know. You'll be thirteen in December.'

'Yes!' said Edie. 'But that is NOT going to happen to me! I'll always be able to see you.'

She spoke with conviction, but uncertainty sat deep in her stomach like a cold pebble.

Chapter Three

Alexandra Park Road

A large cream envelope lay on the kitchen table. It was already specked with toast crumbs and a puddle of blackcurrant jam as Mr Winter had insisted on eating his breakfast first.

'What a mess!' said Mum, pulling on her coat to go to work.

Edie noticed the letter had a French postmark.

She was already dressed for school. Now that she was in Year Eight her uniform didn't feel so scratchy and new any more. Her shoes were nicely scuffed and she no longer wore her hair in plaits, but instead set it loose around her shoulders or strung up in a high ponytail.

'What is it, Dad?' she said.

Mr Winter brushed away the last of the crumbs, his toast burnt just as he liked it, and tore open the envelope.

'Well, this is a surprise,' he said, holding up the letter.

'*Le service des objets trouvés.*' Edie read out the words stamped at the top in halting French. She had just started to learn French at school. 'What does that mean?'

'It's the Lost Property Office for the Paris Metro, just like my office here for the London Underground. The letter is from Madame Cloutier, the *directrice*. I've been invited to visit!' Mr Winter read on. 'They would like to celebrate our success here in London, and they want to make a waxwork of me and put it in a station called Gare du Nord!'

Edie and Mum couldn't help laughing at the thought of a model of Dad cast in wax and standing forever at a busy Parisian station.

It was true that Dad and the London Transport Lost Property Office had achieved quite some notoriety after discovering the haul of hidden valuables in the ghost station at Wilde Street. Even Edie had become relatively famous for a few weeks, with others at school saying, 'Weren't you scared down there in the dark?' and 'Why didn't you keep all that stuff yourself?'

In Lost Property circles everywhere, the London story was admired and passed on.

Is the London Transport's Lost Property Office the best in the world? headlines had blared, and now the Parisians wanted to keep a version of Dad forever and were offering an official visit.

'I've been asked to go the week after next,' Dad went on as he read further down the letter. 'And I'm allowed to bring a small party of guests.' He looked at Mum.

'Well, it's a bit short notice,' she said, pointing at a large poster stuck to the fridge advertising *Jack and the Beanstalk on Ice*. 'That week's half-term and I've got the show. But why don't you take Edie and a friend?'

Mum worked at the ice rink at Alexandra Palace as Head of Events. She had grown up in Finland and was quite happy to spend all day in a Puffa jacket alongside the cold, glassy surface of the skating rink. Once work was finished she would glide effortlessly around several circuits of the rink, with Edie occasionally joining her to wobble along behind.

'Of course, Benedict will have to manage the Lost Property Office while I'm away,' Dad said. Benedict was now Deputy Manager, and to prove it he wore a T-shirt with *Deputy Dawg* emblazoned across the front. 'But, Edie, I'd be only too happy to have you and a friend along,' Dad went on. 'After all, if it wasn't for you, Charlie and Benedict, none of this would have happened.'

Edie flung her arms around Dad's neck. A trip to Paris!

'I expect you'll want to ask Charlie to come with us?' Dad asked.

This pulled her up short.

'Er . . . I don't know about Charlie, Dad. He's always busy with other stuff now. And he's probably got Scout camp over half-term. I think I'll ask someone else.'

Chapter Four

Alexandra Park Road, further along

E die hovered at the end of the pathway leading up to Naz's house. There was a snap in the air and little eddies of dry leaves swirled around her feet. Naz was standing in the doorway with Sami, trying to get her ready for primary school.

'You've got your shoe on the wrong foot!'

Sami hopped about on the doorstep, her arm tangled up in her coat and her book bag spilling onto the pavement.

'Come ON, Sami!' said Naz.

Edie, longing to tell Naz her news, opened the gate and ran up the path.

'Can you come to Paris in half-term?' she said. 'Dad's been asked to go for work, and I can take a friend!' It came out all garbled, but Naz stopped struggling with Sami's shoes and stared at Edie, her eyes like saucers.

'Paris, *France?*' she said.

'Yes!' said Edie. 'Oh, please say you can come!'

'Yesss!' said Naz.

'But you have to look after *me* over half-term!' Sami blurted out, prodding her older sister in the ribs. Mrs Balik had a busy job as a hospital doctor and if Naz went to Paris it meant only one thing . . .

'I'm not going back to Crafty Camp,' Sami said, screwing up her face like a prune. 'Crafty Camp is stupid!'

Sami's Crafty Camp record wasn't good. The previous summer she had stuck her fingers together with glue on the first day, and on the second she had tried to dislodge a box of glitter from a shelf and tipped it upside down. It created a shiny blizzard that blew specks of foil all over the library.

'I won't go!' Sami said, stamping her 'one-shoe' foot.

'I'll talk to Mum,' Naz said hurriedly and whispered to Edie, 'I'm sure it'll be fine!' She turned back to Sami and jammed the missing shoe on the other foot.

'Come *on*, Sami, or we'll be late!'

As they walked down the road, Sami seemed to forget all about Crafty Camp and she jigged around in front of Edie.

'Can I come to see the flits again this week? Please! I've got some things for their camp.'

'She put all our eggs in the bread bin so she could

give the flits the egg boxes,' whispered Naz. 'And swapped her Pokémon cards for some LEGO bricks with the boy next door.'

Edie had to smile at Sami's persistence. 'OK. You can come with us,' she said. 'But don't forget what I said, Sami. It's our secret!'

Sami nodded and launched into a list of questions. 'Do all flits fly?'

'Not all. You saw Nid. He just jumps everywhere.'

'Can adults see them?'

'No,' said Edie, trying not to think about Charlie.

'How did you meet them again?'

Naz laughed. 'Mum and I think Sami's going to be a detective!'

Edie took a deep breath. They had reached the busy main road that ran alongside the school playground and the story of how she first met the flits was long and tangled.

'Well, you know that my dad runs the Lost Property Office for London Transport?'

Sami nodded, her eyes fixed on Edie.

'I found a box on the Bakerloo Line, an abandoned box, and some flits were inside. They needed my help, as someone called Vera Creech was capturing them and training them to be pickpockets on the Underground.'

'I thought you said only children could see them!'

Why *so* many questions? Edie thought, as they stepped out to cross the busy road.

'Yes, that's right. Only Vera had a special eyeglass, which meant she could see them.'

'Where's the eyeglass now?' Sami asked over the traffic.

'We don't know what happened to it,' Edie said.

'Too many questions, Sami! You don't want to be late,' said Naz.

Sami grinned at them both and ran through the school gates. It was the same school where Naz and Edie had met right back in Reception, sitting side by side, cross-legged on the floor. At the doorway, Sami turned back and called out to Edie, 'See you later!'

Edie nodded and Sami gave a final thumbs-up as she disappeared inside. Naz slipped her arm through Edie's as they walked on up towards the purpose-built buildings of the secondary school. A steady stream of new Year Sevens walked past them, their uniforms still clean and pressed. Edie remembered the difficult feelings she had felt last year, when she had been a new Year Seven and thought that all her old friends had deserted her. School had seemed like an alien planet then, but now its corridors were no longer a maze and the voices of a thousand children ricocheting off the walls as they moved between classrooms was less overwhelming. With Naz beside her, Edie felt her confidence flooding back as she passed the huddles of other Year Eights dotted around the recreation area. At every break they sat together and talked about the teachers, giggling helplessly at Mr Binding's short trousers and grimacing at the endless maths homework. Linny, who had been so unfriendly to Edie the year before, looked over and scowled at them most days as if it was she who was now missing out on the party.

*

That night Mrs Balik phoned and Edie could hear Dad discussing the trip to France with her. From the half of the conversation she could hear, it sounded like Mrs Balik was saying yes, Naz would love to go with them, but Sami was a problem. What to do?

Leave Sami behind to do half-term activities! Edie thought to herself, but Dad was very sympathetic to the anti-Crafty Camp sentiment and wrote immediately to the Lost Property Office in Paris to accept their invitation and to ask if he could bring a 'junior' along as a fourth guest.

It was not what Naz and Edie wanted, but Dad insisted on it to help Mrs Balik.

If Naz was coming, then so was Sami.

Chapter Five

St Pancras International to Gare du Nord

The huge arched ceiling of St Pancras International station soared over them like the ribs of a giant whale. Mr Winter had taken them upstairs to see the gleaming blue-and-silver Eurostar train waiting to depart from the upper platform.

'It looks like a javelin,' Naz said, who was keen on athletics.

Mrs Balik and Benedict had come to wave them off through the ticket barriers down below. Benedict was wearing his leather jacket and, instead of his white *Deputy Dawg* T-shirt, he was wearing a blue one stamped with the words *Vive la France*. The Paris train was called and Mr Winter handed him the keys to the Lost Property Office. In return Benedict gave them a list of Paris Metro stations entitled *Interesting Metro Stations to Visit*.

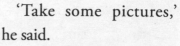

'Take some pictures,' he said.

Mrs Balik adjusted the straps of Sami's rucksack as she said goodbye, telling Naz that she mustn't let Sami out of her sight. Dad herded them through customs, helping them to feed their luggage through the X-ray machines and skirt around passengers pulling wheelie suitcases behind them as they all moved towards passport control.

Within the first hour, the Eurostar train had glided out of London through Kent and had slid effortlessly into the thirty-one-mile tunnel that runs under the English Channel. The lights flickered on and Mr Winter thumbed through a guidebook.

'The tunnel is so long that you could stack 169 Eiffel Towers top to tail along the tracks,' he said as they barrelled through.

'Mum showed us a picture of the Eiffel Tower last night,' said Naz.

Edie peered out of the window. She imagined the gallons of English Channel sea water overhead, choppy and green, and she could make out the long, trailing cables and the brickwork of the tunnel walls just as she had done in the London Underground when Nid had gone missing.

Twenty minutes later it was daylight again and they were in France. The landscape already seemed very different – wide, flat fields and farmland with big skies, electricity pylons and houses with red-tiled roofs. Edie had only been to Finland on a plane to see her grandmother, Granny Agata, and Naz and Sami had barely left London as nearly all their extended family lived there. This was the first time any of them had been to France.

Sami was surprisingly quiet during the journey. She looked thoughtfully out of the window and kept her hands in her pocket.

Naz whispered, 'I hope she's not ill!'

The train pulled into Gare du Nord and they stepped out onto the platform. Two porters were calling to one another and a family bustled past. The language they spoke was different – much faster and more expressive – to the plodding French they practised in class. Even the air smelt different. It reminded Edie of hot chestnuts and fresh bread.

Dad walked on ahead, but as Edie, Naz and Sami moved towards the barriers and were queueing to move through, Sami bent down and said in a loud whisper, 'Nearly there!' She seemed to be addressing her coat pocket.

Naz looked at her and her eyes narrowed. 'Sami? Who were you talking to?'

'My friend!'

Sami dipped her hand into her pocket and pulled out a matchbox. She carefully pushed the inner box out and inside, lying on a cotton-wool pillow and kicking her legs, was Pea.

Edie felt panicked. She remembered that Sami had run back to the flits camp the evening before at the last minute to 'say goodnight' to Pea, lingering behind as the deserted station grew dark.

'Sami! You stole Pea.'

'Oh no,' said Sami. 'I didn't steal her! She wanted to come with me.' Pea sat up and wildly clapped her hands in the matchbox.

'But what about Flum!'

'I left a note for her,' Sami said cheerfully. 'I wrote, *Pea is safe!*'

'But Impy and Nid will be really worried,' Edie said.

'I knew *that*,' Sami said. 'So I brought them along too. I put them in a sock with some boiled sweets.' She pulled a knotted sock out of her rucksack and already Edie could hear Impy's familiar agitated voice. She untied it and Impy came whirring upwards. A bit of boiled sweet was stuck to her hair and, just as Naz did too, she had the look of a furious big sister. Nid stayed in the toe of the sock, clutching a lemon sherbet and ignoring everyone.

'She took Pea!' Impy exploded. 'And put us in that sock with a sticky sweet!'

'Sami, how could you!' Edie said.

'Keep up, Edie,' called Dad from further down the platform.

Edie and Naz looked at each other. It was not at all how they had imagined it. They now had Sami *and* three flits to take care of in a city they didn't know.

Chapter Six

Hotel Esmeralda

The Paris Lost Property Office had arranged for them all to stay at the Hotel Esmeralda, on the banks of the River Seine. A rickety staircase led up to an attic room, and a camp bed was set up in between Naz and Edie's beds for Sami. Dad had a room at the back of the hotel. Bright red wallpaper with clumps of white blossom was pasted all over the walls, doorways and ceiling, as if someone had wrapped up the room like a present.

'Isn't France brilliant!' said Naz, pushing open the windows and gazing out at the River Seine and the bridge that crossed over it to the cathedral of Notre Dame.

But Edie still felt anxious and the wallpaper was beginning to give her a headache. Nid was swinging from the curtain braids, Sami was organising a paddling pool for Pea in a soap dish and Impy was complaining about the whole adventure.

Edie had hastily made a temporary camp for the flits on the dressing table and Impy was sitting cross-legged on a hotel teabag, sulking.

'Well, we're here now,' said Edie.

'I know *that*.'

'It might be fun to see Paris.'

'For you maybe . . . but I'll probably be stuck here taking care of Pea.'

Edie had already thought of this, weighing up the risk of all venturing out together or leaving the flits behind in the hotel room where Pea might fall out of the window or slip down a plughole. 'I'd like you to come with us,' she said firmly.

'Really?' said Impy, visibly brightening.

'But you have to stay hidden in my pocket, Impy.'

'Ugh!' said Impy. 'It's stuffy in there.'

'It's too dangerous otherwise! There might be Parisian cats with sharp claws that catch flits, or rats that eat you for breakfast or, even worse, adults who can see you.'

Impy, who was as brave as a giant, gave a slight shiver at the thought.

*

They were due for a formal welcome with Dad the next morning at the Lost Property Office in Rue des Morillons so they had time that afternoon to explore the city on their own. Dad proposed a tour of the Paris Metro, visiting the stations on Benedict's list. They met in the hotel lobby, with Impy hidden in Edie's top pocket. Pea was inside a matchbox in Sami's pocket and Nid was zipped into the front of Naz's rucksack. Edie had once again lectured all three flits on the dangers of French cats with sharp claws and made them promise to stay out of sight.

'Don't let *anyone* see the flits until we know it's safe,' Edie whispered to Sami sternly.

Dad was holding a French phrasebook, Benedict's list and a large map of the Paris Metro.

'This way!' he said, leading them out into a cobbled street beside a small square of green outside the hotel. They walked over the bridge, looking down at the grey-green thread of the River Seine and through a flower market to the Metro station at Cité.

The steps down to the Metro were framed by delicate, curling Art Nouveau ironwork and green lettering.

'Metro-poli-tain,' read Naz.

Down in the station itself the platforms were lit by huge globe lanterns that arched over them making it look a bit like a ballroom. Edie had to admit that the Paris Metro already felt more airy and glamorous than the London Underground that she loved so much.

Dad chatted loudly about the trains, marvelling at the detail – the big rubber wheels, the spring catches on the doors, and the carriages, which were much squarer and more box-like than their London counterparts. Sami liked the brightly coloured bucket seats on the platforms and Edie and Naz just loved hearing the horn that sounded every time the train left a station. They all liked the smooth hiss the rubber wheels made as the trains travelled between stations, as it was so different to the rattle and whine of the Piccadilly Line. Naz thought it sounded like seawash on a beach and Edie thought it was like fishfingers frying in a pan.

'*Allons-y!*' Dad said confidently, having checked

the French guidebook as they changed onto Line 1 at Châtelet. Edie knew enough French to know that '*allons-y*' meant 'let's go!'

The first station on Benedict's list was Louvre Rivoli, which was the stop for the famous art gallery above. Softly lit classical statues stood in alcoves along the platforms next to glass cabinets displaying Egyptian figures. Standing on the platform felt as if you were in a corridor in a museum. At Concorde the walls of the station were covered in blue-and-white tiles with letters on them to form a giant French word-search puzzle.

Naz's favourite was Arts et Métiers. It was designed by a comic artist and looked like a submarine with copper walls and shiny bolts and portholes. Dad bounced up and down the platform in the warm amber glow, taking pictures to show Benedict and the staff back at the Lost Property Office in London. Edie could see that Sami was holding Pea in her fist, opening her fingers slightly so that Pea could peep through the gap, and Nid's head popped in and out of the zipped front pocket of Naz's rucksack as if he was a submarine periscope, but Edie felt like an anxious parent, and whenever Impy squeezed herself out of Edie's pocket to look, she gently pushed her back inside.

They sat at the front of a driverless train on the way to Bastille so that they could see the track unravel in front of them and the tunnels strung with cables and dotted with lights. The train ran out into the open air and drew up at Bastille. The walls of the station were like the best kind of history lesson, with painted scenes from the French Revolution over 230 years earlier where a battle had taken place in the street above and revolutionaries had stormed the prison.

There was a lull between trains and Edie and Naz stood a little away from the others and leant against the tiled wall. Dad was giving Sami a crash course in the French Revolution further down the platform.

'Nid! Where are you going?' Naz said, looking down at her rucksack.

At the edge of the platform was a small open gutter or drain and Nid had jumped down into it. He was foraging for pieces of French rubbish and he'd spied a twenty-cent euro coin wedged down the back and a caramel sweet wrapped in shiny gold foil. Lifting them into his arms, he ran to and fro between the rucksack and the gutter until all this booty was stored. Then he paused, and, jumping up and down, he pointed at something further along the guttering.

'What is it?' said Edie.

A tiny bell rang and something shot past so fast that it was nothing more than a blur. Impy squeezed herself out of Edie's pocket and flew down onto the ground beside Nid before Edie could stop her. Once again there was a flash, a strange disturbance of air, as something scooted past and into a pipe under some steps. Edie looked at Naz.

'What was that?'

Nid jumped down into the drain, ready to run after whatever it was.

'Nid!' hissed Edie, and Impy flew down after him and grabbed his jacket.

'What are you looking at?' said Dad, who had wandered over to where they were sitting.

'Nothing much!' said Edie. She could see that Impy was dragging Nid back into Naz's rucksack and Naz firmly zipped up the pocket once they were both inside. A train drew in and Edie and Naz followed Dad onboard and sat down on the flip seats. They felt like exhausted parents already.

'What was it?' said Edie.

'I don't know,' said Naz. 'Maybe mice?'

'I don't think it was mice,' Edie replied.

Chapter Seven

Hotel Esmeralda to Rue des Morillons

'Do you think they were *flits*?' she asked Impy as they got ready for their visit to the Paris Lost Property Office the next morning. Dad had insisted that they all dress formally and she was lacing up her school shoes.

'I couldn't really see,' said Impy. 'They went by so fast! But Nid thinks that whatever they were, they had wheels!' Nid seemed thrilled by the 'flash-past' in the drain at Bastille and made wild circular actions with his arms as he settled into Naz's rucksack.

'You will have to watch him,' Edie said to Impy as she slipped her into her pocket.

Dad had squeezed himself into a wool suit that already looked uncomfortably hot by the time they had reached the local Metro station. And Edie could feel her school shoes beginning to pinch her toes.

As they walked down Rue des Morillons they could see bunting in red, white and blue pinned up across the doorway. A boy bounced up to them.

'Hello,' he said in English. 'Are you Monsieur Winter and party?'

'We certainly are,' said Dad, dabbing at his forehead with a large hanky.

'This way,' said the boy and he darted away from them back down the street.

As they approached the entrance to the Lost Property Office, right on cue, a small brass band that was seated around the doorway launched into the French National Anthem. Dad, much to Edie's embarrassment, began to march in time to the music. She could see the French boy leaning against the wall watching them, and he seemed to be laughing, but he was holding his hand up to his face to hide it. She wondered if it was because of Dad's marching, and she immediately decided she didn't like him. She gave him a stony stare as they drew alongside him.

A small woman wearing wide trousers and a red blazer was waiting for them on the doorstep. The music ended and she opened her arms out like a fan.

'Mister Winter!' she said. 'I am Isabelle Cloutier – the *directrice*.' She adjusted her blazer and launched into a speech.

'It is my pleasure to welcome you to *le service des objets trouvés* – our very own Parisian Lost Property Office.'

As the speech went on, Edie's concentration began to wander and she looked over to the boy who was now standing behind the brass band. He was frowning and kicking his heel against the wall. Then, as suddenly as Madame Cloutier had started, she stopped and the brass band broke into a fanfare.

'Please follow me,' said Madame Cloutier, and she held up a small French flag. 'This way.'

They turned and followed her through a large reception room. A few people sat perched on wooden seats clutching envelopes and waiting to be called up to the desk. An elderly woman had just been reunited with a large handbag that had been missing for several weeks, and she was marvelling that it still had a twenty-euro note and her packet of mint humbugs inside.

'We date back to the time of Napoleon!' Madame Cloutier called over her shoulder as she led them down into the basement. Just as in Dad's Lost Property Office in London, they found themselves in a huge underground warehouse with aisles of grey, metal shelving.

'Well, this is splendid!' said Dad, feeling quite at home in among the huge shelves packed with coats and hats, forgotten wallets, keys and mobile phones.

Here each item was wrapped in white paper, fastened with an elastic band and given a number.

Madame Cloutier beamed with pride and started a detailed discussion with Dad about alphabetical labelling.

Edie and Naz, with Sami held firmly between them, wandered behind, looking for things that might be distinctly French. The hats and scarves and shoes were much the same as the ones in the London office, if a little more tailored. There was a motor scooter helmet and some tennis racquets, a set of boules, a biscuit tin and a large French flag furled up. One shelf was covered in fridge magnets of the Eiffel Tower and the seaside towns of the South of France.

'Look, Sami!' said Naz, holding up a stuffed grey elephant wearing a green suit and a crown. 'Babar!' She turned to Edie. 'Mum used to read the stories to us.'

'Can I show Pea?' said Sami in a loud whisper. Both Edie and Naz shook their heads, and as they were at the back of the guided tour Edie quickly slipped Impy into Sami's pocket with Pea to make sure that Pea remained hidden.

'We keep everything for four months,' Madame Cloutier was saying. 'And then we shred all the important documents and melt the keys down for scrap metal.'

They reached the far end of the aisle where Madame

Cloutier came to an abrupt stop. A large glass cabinet stood in a corner displaying a ship in a bottle, a silver pin box and a faded wedding dress. A sword with a curved blade hung on the wall and a replica Parisian streetlamp, which must have been from a theatre or a film set, stood beside them on the floor looking a bit like the one that Mr Tumnus stood under in the snowy landscape of Narnia.

'To lose a wedding dress seems a bit forgetful!' said Dad, looking at the faded lacework.

'This corner is our Musée de l'Insolite,' said Madame Cloutier to her visitors. 'In English I think this means it is our "Museum of the Strange".'

'Dad! It's just like the Storeroom at the End,' Edie couldn't help blurting out. The Storeroom at the End was the room in Baker Street where odd missing items that couldn't be easily categorised were placed. It was where Edie had first encountered the flits inside their abandoned box.

Naz had walked on and was staring at a glass dome set on a wooden plinth that contained a single iridescent blue butterfly. Edie joined her and, looking more closely, they could see that the butterfly was pinned to a fake branch fashioned out of cork with tiny leaves made of green silk stitched onto it. The colours were vibrant, but the whole scene had no life to it.

'I don't like it,' said Naz.

'This only arrived yesterday,' said Madame Cloutier, tapping a varnished red fingernail on the glass.

'I know who that belongs to!' said a voice behind them.

It was the annoying boy from the street. Close up, Edie could see that the boy was maybe a year younger than her. His hair was swept back from his head as if he might have flown at speed down the stairs to the basement, and when he smiled you could see all his teeth.

'Ah, this is my grandson, Fabien,' said Madame Cloutier. 'He helps me when he can, as he has a keen eye. He would like to be a detective . . . or so he says.'

'I would too,' said Sami.

'Like Sherlock Holmes of Baker Street,' said Dad. 'He's a neighbour to our Lost Property Office in Baker Street in London. Or I should say, he *was* – over a hundred years ago!'

'Yes! I know Sherlock Holmes,' said Fabien. He didn't seem to be very impressed, and Edie could see that Dad looked a little crushed. Fabien went on: 'He lived at 221B Baker Street.'

His English, like his grandmother's, was very fluent.

'He didn't *really* live there. It was only in the stories,' Edie whispered to Naz.

If Fabien heard this, he chose to ignore it and instead pulled a small torch out of his pocket. He carefully tipped the glass dome with the butterfly upside down and pointed to the bottom of the plinth.

'Look!' Fabien said.

Under the beam of light they could all see that there was a tiny label with a stamp. *Victor Rottier – La Maison de Verre, Passage de Curiosité.*

Chapter Eight

Rue des Morillons

'Ah, so it belongs to the Glass House Man!' said Madame Cloutier. 'Bravo, Fabien! Tomorrow, as it is a school holiday, you must return it in person. And perhaps . . . our young English friends would like to go with you?' She generously swept her arm across Naz, Edie and Sami.

Edie wasn't at all sure she wanted to go on a Lost Property delivery round with Fabien. He seemed to think he knew everything, and anyway, she did deliveries like that all the time in London.

'The Glass House Man is quite famous in Paris. He's a proper artist!' said Fabien.

'Well spotted, Fabien!' said Dad. 'You should come and work for us.'

Edie felt fidgety and cross. Why had Dad suggested that Fabien come and work in London when that was her place? And he was younger than her. But Fabien's reply wasn't what she expected.

'No, thanks,' said Fabien. 'I like it here.'

Madame Cloutier looked a little embarrassed by her grandson's blunt answer. 'I think Fabien would enjoy working with you very much,' she said reassuringly. The disembodied voice of one of the reception staff upstairs called for her over the tannoy and she went off to answer it.

Edie looked at Fabien. Was he jealous of them all? She couldn't work him out, and now that he had been rude to Dad she liked him even less.

Dad seemed absorbed in the sword with the curved blade hanging on the wall and Fabien didn't apologise. Instead, he had pulled a Metro map out of his pocket and was showing Naz where the Glass House Man's shop was and explaining how the Metro lines worked.

'Every Metro line has a number. So this is Line 11 and then you look for the station at the end of the line to know which way you're travelling.' Fabien was tracing his finger along the map. Edie put on a 'bored face', although no one seemed to notice.

'So starting at Châtelet, Line 11 goes along here through Hotel de Ville, Rambuteau, Arts et Métiers – that's a brilliant station as it's all copper and like a submarine.'

'Yes! We've seen it!' said Naz.

Why was Naz even listening to him? thought Edie.

'It's my favourite Metro station so far,' Naz added.

'Have you ever been on the Piccadilly Line?' Edie asked Fabien abruptly.

Fabien and Naz looked at her.

'I have never been to London, so *non*!' said Fabien.

'The Piccadilly Line has fifty-three stations,' Edie went on. 'But that's not the highest number. The District Line (which is coloured green) has the most, and the longest is the Central Line (which is red), and Waterloo has the most escalators.' This all came out in a long and bossy list.

Fabien looked bewildered and Naz was frowning slightly.

'Can you spell Piccadilly?' Edie asked, with a defiant note in her voice.

'Fabien hasn't even *been* to London,' Naz said. 'Didn't you hear him?'

'He knew where Sherlock Holmes lived. So why can't he spell Piccadilly?' Edie said crossly. For the first time she felt that Naz was being critical of her.

'*Everyone* knows where Sherlock Holmes lived!' said Fabien. There was a short silence.

'Edie, you know all the London Underground stuff because of my job,' said Dad, who had rejoined them and was listening in. 'How about you try to spell some of the Parisian stations on Line 11. Like . . . Rambuteau, for instance?'

Edie got as far as R-O, which was the wrong spelling, and stopped. Naz gave her a funny look and Edie looked at the floor.

'Mr Winter, would you like to see how we catalogue everything on our database?' Madame Cloutier called. She had dealt with the call on the tannoy.

'Edie, remember we're here as invited guests,' said Dad quietly and walked off after her.

Edie felt her cheeks flare. She knew that she had overreacted and been unreasonable to Fabien and her annoyance had spilled out and they had all seen it. Naz and Fabien turned away from her and carried on looking at the map, so Edie felt in her pocket for Impy for reassurance. Then she remembered that Impy was with Pea and she glanced back down the racks to look for Sami, who had been trailing behind. But Sami had disappeared.

'I'm just going to find Sami,' she said.

She walked a little way back and spotted Sami down an aisle that led off at right angles from the main shelves. She was in among the section that contained missing toys. The Babar elephant was propped up where Naz had left him, alongside a baby's striped rabbit with a chewed ear, a racing car and a plastic pull-along duck. Sami was at the end of the row looking at what appeared to be a small, open suitcase. She held her arm out in front of her and, as Edie came up alongside her, she could see that both Impy and Pea were standing up on the palm of her hand.

'Sami! Be careful! Pea should be in your pocket. You shouldn't be so careless.'

Sami breezily ignored Edie's warning. 'Look, Edie! It's a shop in a suitcase!'

She pushed the lid further back to reveal a miniature grocer's shop. It looked old and dusty, as if it had belonged to someone's great-grandmother and been handed down as a family heirloom. The plaster figure of a grocer stood in front of some scales and behind him were bottles and jars, a pink ham on a plate and tiny packets of French biscuits. Pea ran forward and tried to pick up an orange from a box on the counter, but it was hard and made of paste.

'It's not real!' Sami said, but Pea took no notice and walked into the shop as if she was out on an errand. She tried to pull out a packet of biscuits. Impy followed her inside.

Edie couldn't help feeling drawn to the scene before her, but her prickly feelings were still swimming around inside. She felt as if everyone was pushing her away to the margins and wasn't taking any notice of her.

'Impy, why won't you listen to me!' she said. 'It's dangerous! Come back here.'

Impy turned back very slowly and looked at Edie. 'You're being bossy. That's why,' she said flatly. 'And maybe Sami isn't trying to smother us, or stuff us in her boring pocket all the time like you do.'

Edie felt as if she had been punched in the ribs. It was a body blow. Fabien was the boring one, not her!

'I'm just trying to keep you safe,' she said primly.

Impy stalked off around the side of the case where a miniature bicycle was propped up against the wall. Unlike the shop, the bicycle looked shiny and new. It had a silver frame with a small leather seat and a basket on the front, in which there was a tiny baguette.

Impy wheeled the bicycle out and pedalled it up and down, ringing the tiny bicycle bell with joyful abandon, almost to taunt Edie. Then stopping, she pulled the baguette out of the basket and looked puzzled.

'It's real bread,' she said and, breaking it in half, she gave a chunk to Pea.

'It's still warm! And there's cheese inside.'

She broke off another piece and gave it to Sami. Holding the crumb between her thumb and forefinger, Sami popped it in her mouth.

'It's like fresh bread.'

This was strange, Edie thought. The grocer's shop

was a toy, battered and dusty and old, and all the items were made of clay or paste. She stared again at the plaster figure of the grocer with the cracked arm, but he didn't move.

'Ee-die?'

Edie could hear Naz calling. They must be coming this way.

'Quick!' she said. 'We can't let Fabien see you.'

This time the others took note. Pea hopped back onto Sami's hand, still clutching the crust of bread, and Impy hurriedly wheeled the bicycle back into place.

Sami was just about to close up the case when a cupboard behind the plaster grocer flew open and a tiny figure, with a pan stolen from the grocer's shop strapped to its back, ran across the counter and round the side to grab the bicycle.

They all stared as the figure cycled furiously along the shelf and up a ramp at the back by the wall. The ramp led up to a pipe that had a loose joint so that one part of the pipe was open-mouthed and dangling downwards.

'Wait!' cried Impy, running after the cyclist. 'Hello! Who are you?' Whoever it was had ridden into the entrance of the pipe and disappeared.

'Impy!' hissed Edie, but Impy had clambered up inside the pipe after the cyclist.

'Here you are!' said Naz, who was now only a few metres away with Fabien. Sami quickly closed the matchbox with Pea inside and stuffed her hand in her pocket. Naz stood in front of them, not seeming to find anything odd about Edie's and Sami's fixed expressions. Instead she held up a ten-euro note.

'Look what Madame Cloutier has given us,' she said. 'Fabien is going to take us to choose some cakes!' She took Edie's hand for a moment, trying to make amends.

'Are you OK?'

With Fabien watching, all Edie could do was give a very small nod.

Naz smiled happily and turned back down the aisle. 'Come on then!'

Edie hadn't forgotten about the awkward scene only moments before, but her thoughts were now crowded out with worries about getting Impy back and not letting Fabien suspect anything. Even if there were flits in Paris, he was probably too busy showing off to even see them. Hoping that they wouldn't be gone for long, she gave one last desperate scan of the shelf and didn't notice that Fabien was looking curiously at Sami's pocket.

Chapter Nine

Rue des Morillons to Patisserie Bernard

'How long will we be?' Edie asked for the third time. They stood in a row looking in the window of the patisserie. She had measured the distance to the shop in footsteps, working out that if they ate the cakes quickly they might only be away for half an hour. She had to get back and find out what had happened to Impy.

It was a corner shop just a few minutes from the Paris Lost Property Office and it had gold lettering over the door. In the window was the most beautiful display of cakes Edie had ever seen. A line of decorated chocolate éclairs filled with cream sat next to perfect circles of pastry topped with glossy strawberries. Alongside that were tarts filled with citrus-yellow lemon curd, tiny madeleines of light sponge and neat rows of rectangular cakes with delicate layers of cream and pastry.

'It's as if an artist has made them all!' said Naz.

'Can you actually eat them?' Sami asked.

'Of course!' said Fabien, laughing. 'Choose one each.'

They sat outside the café at two small iron tables. Edie had chosen an éclair with specks of gold leaf on the slick of dark chocolate.  When she bit into the éclair, it was so light that she felt as if she was eating a cloud. She folded a large chunk of sticky choux pastry into a tissue and slipped it into her pocket for Impy. She wanted to say sorry for being so bossy.

Naz had chosen a tart and already had lemon curd all over her face, and Sami had ordered a sugared doughnut filled with blackcurrant jam but had left it sitting on a plate on the table.

'Are you not going to eat it?' said Fabien.

'I'm saving it for my friend.'

'Your friend?' said Fabien, looking confused.

Edie glared at her. She knew in that moment that Sami was not going to be able to keep their secret. Sami took no notice of Edie's expression and, turning her back on them all, she plunged her hand into her pocket and brought out the matchbox, setting it on the table beside her patisserie.

'No, Sami,' hissed Naz. 'Not here!' She put her hand over the matchbox. They sat in silence for a few minutes with Naz looking awkward with her outstretched hand. Once again Fabien looked at them curiously.

'Does your friend live in a matchbox?' he asked Sami.

'It's just an imaginary friend,' Naz said quickly.

'No, it's *not*!' said Sami. 'And Edie has –'

'Sami!' said Naz, cutting her short. 'Stop being an idiot! Fabien doesn't want to know.' They sat in silence for a few seconds more with Sami visibly sulking, her shoulders hunched over her as-yet-uneaten doughnut.

Finally Fabien stood up. 'I have something I have to do,' he said.

'Will it take long?' Edie asked. She desperately wanted to get back to Rue des Morillons. 'I mean . . . we should probably be getting back to Dad.'

'No, it won't take long. I'll be back in a few minutes.' He left the table and walked up the alleyway beside the patisserie.

With Fabien gone, Edie immediately said to Naz, 'I have to tell you something.' But Naz was distracted by Sami, who was tugging furiously at her hand and prising open her fingers. She managed to pull the matchbox out from under it and, sliding it open, she allowed Pea to jump out.

'Look, Pea! We're at a French cake shop!'

Pea stood beside the doughnut, which towered above her like a giant stuffed pillow, and began dabbing her finger in the sugar crystals with a delighted squeal. All Edie could think was that Sami's determination to show Pea everything was going to get them into trouble.

'Sami, I told you . . .' began Naz, as she and Edie tried to shield the table from passers-by.

Pea's fluted voice cut across hers. 'Nid! Impy! There's cake!'

It only took seconds for Nid to unzip part of the pocket on Naz's rucksack and clamber up the table leg beside her. He made a running dive for the lemon tart, scooping the deliciously sticky curd into his mouth with both hands. Of course, there was no sign of Impy.

'Impy's missing!' Sami said suddenly, remembering what had happened in the Lost Property Office.

'Missing?' said Naz.

'I've been trying to tell you,' said Edie. 'We saw something – another small person on a bicycle.'

'It looked like a flit,' said Sami, raising her voice.

'Sssh, Sami!' said Edie. 'We don't know that for sure, but whatever it was, Impy ran after it. We have to get back to the Lost Property Office as quickly as we can.

Can you make sure the flits are hidden and I'll keep a lookout for Fabien?'

Naz nodded and Edie walked over to the bottom of the alleyway that Fabien had taken. It ran along the side of the bakery and Edie walked a little way up to stand guard, pausing by a large sliding kitchen door that was half open. Gusts of warm, sweet air blew through it, smelling of freshly baked bread and pastries, and Edie could hear voices inside speaking in French. One of them sounded like Fabien.

Pressing herself against the wall, she glanced around the side of the doorway and could see a rack of shiny ovens and trays of pastry cases ready to go in. Fabien was in the kitchen hovering beside a huge mixing bowl filled with dough that was sitting just under the window. Edie drew back so that she was hidden from view and watched Fabien through a crack in the door. He was talking to a baker in the kitchen. The man moved over to a rack to fill a bag with fresh croissants for Fabien but, as his back was turned, Fabien took two thimbles from his pocket and dipped them into the dough in the mixing bowl, then returned them to his pocket. Why would he do that? she wondered.

The man handed the bag of croissants to Fabien and Edie turned to run back down the alleyway to warn the others he was coming, but she caught her foot and slipped and fell, grazing her knee. Fabien came out of the bakery to find her sprawled on the cobbles.

'Edie, are you OK?' He helped her up. 'Maybe you have three feet!' he added with a toothy grin.

'I don't,' said Edie indignantly.

Fabien looked at her. 'Why are you so cross? It was only a joke.'

'I'm not cross,' said Edie. 'You just think you know everything and it's annoying.' They looked at each other, their dislike evident in their scowls.

'So what were you doing up here behind the bakery?' Fabien asked. 'Were you following me?'

'No, I . . . Well, I might have been.'

'It's rude to follow people! *I'm* supposed to be showing *you* around,' said Fabien. 'As your dad said, you are our so-called "guests",' he added dismissively. 'I don't even know why you *are* here anyway, to be honest.'

This confirmed everything that Edie thought. He *was* jealous.

'You're the rude one,' Edie said. 'You laughed at my dad and then you said you wouldn't come to London.'

'I didn't mean to say it like that,' said Fabien. 'But why is everyone making such a fuss of him and making a stupid waxwork?'

'Because the London Lost Property Office is *famous*,' Edie said. 'More famous than your one here. And it was your grandmother who asked Dad to come here to have the waxwork made.'

Edie turned and walked as fast as she could back down the alleyway ahead of Fabien, trying to ignore her stinging knee.

Chapter Ten

Patisserie Bernard to **Rue des Morillons**

'He's coming,' Edie said angrily as she joined the others. The flits were nowhere to be seen and the matchbox was back in Sami's pocket. Fabien came around the corner of the alley.

'Let's go,' he said, not looking at Edie and setting off at high speed. 'I have to give this to the staff at the Lost Property Office.' He held up the bag of croissants.

Edie was beginning to realise that Fabien ran everywhere, sprinting over cobbles and weaving around pedestrians on the pavement. She, Naz and Sami ran behind in a ragged line, with Edie limping slightly, until they turned into Rue des Morillons. Fabien led them around the back of the Lost Property Office and down some outside steps to a back door. As Fabien opened it they were greeted by a small ball of white fur vigorously barking and jumping up and down as if his paws were on springs.

'This is Napoleon,' said Fabien, lifting him up. 'He's the office guard dog. My grandmother called him Napoleon after the great French general – who was also not very tall.'

Napoleon's tiny pink tongue licked Fabien's ears and his tail wagged furiously.

'He's not very scary!' said Sami. She held out her arms and Napoleon immediately leapt into them and licked her all over her face.

'He wouldn't hurt a fly,' said Fabien. 'But he barks a lot and he is very good with his nose!' Fabien tapped his own nose at Sami. 'I think you say he's a good . . . sniffer?'

Naz and Sami laughed but, as if to demonstrate, Napoleon pressed his nose into Sami's pocket where Pea was hidden in her matchbox.

Could Napoleon smell flits? Edie thought fleetingly.

But she didn't have time to worry about that.

'I've left something down in the storerooms,' she said briskly to Fabien. 'Can you look after Sami for us?' Without waiting for Fabien's answer, she grabbed Naz's hand, dragging her back outside the way they had come – into the reception area and down the stairs into the basement. She desperately wanted to be alone with Naz and not speak to Fabien.

'Edie, you're being quite weird,' said Naz as they walked quickly through the aisles of missing items. 'Fabien's OK.'

'I don't like him,' Edie said.

'Why not?' said Naz.

'He was rude to Dad,' said Edie. 'And he laughed at his marching.'

'I don't think he meant to be rude,' said Naz. 'And the marching was quite funny! Anyway, *you* were really rude back there.'

Edie knew that right at that moment she couldn't give a reasonable answer to that, and she didn't want to get into an argument with Naz, so instead she said, 'Naz, I don't care about Fabien right now. I know I was an idiot earlier and I'm sorry and I was cross with Impy too and now she's run off somewhere to try to prove a point. Everything's going wrong and it's my fault. What if something's happened to Impy?'

Naz said nothing but took her hand and squeezed it. They found the toy aisle and the shelf with Babar the elephant and the suitcase shop and Edie rummaged around behind it. The small bicycle was nowhere to be seen and neither was Impy.

Pulling herself up so that she was leaning across the shelf near the ramp, she called into the opening of the pipe, 'Imm-peee! Imp-eeee!' Her voice reverberated through the pipes, sounding tinny and desperate. There was no reply.

'She might be lost forever in there,' said Edie. 'Perhaps

she's met a rat or slid down into a sewer!' The word 'sewer' caught in her throat.

'Maybe Nid can help,' said Naz, unzipping her rucksack. Nid appeared, still sticky with lemon curd, and Naz lifted him out and put him down at the top of the ramp by the entrance to the loose pipe. 'He's the only one that can find her if she's in there.'

'Good plan,' said Edie.

They told Nid what had happened and had to restrain him from immediately rushing inside the pipe to look for his sister. Edie asked him if he had anything he could bang on the side to let them know where he was. Nid pointed at a loose nail lying on the shelf. He held the nail in one hand like a hammer and he also had a tiny pen torch that he held in the other like a spear.

'Bang the nail as hard as you can on the sides of the pipe so that we know where you are.'

Nid did a cartwheel and gave a small salute before clambering inside the old pipe. He gave a *clink-clink* on the sides to tell them where he was in there. They waited until they heard another *clink* further down the wall of the storeroom.

'I hope he finds her!' said Edie anxiously. She had visions of both of them disappearing forever into a network of pipes that ran under Paris, and how she would have to return to the Hillside Camp, to Jot,

Speckle and Flum, with only Pea.

Together they followed Nid's *clink-clinks* around the storeroom as he hammered the nail against the sides of the pipe.

'He's here!' said Naz, running ahead to the shelves of mobile phones.

'Ssssh! Listen. Now he's over here!' said Edie, following the line of the wall and sprinting past piles of coats and hats. The metallic hammering turned a corner and led them both along the far wall of the big basement storeroom, and then there was silence. They listened hard. Nid's clinking was such a small sound that it seemed to have been swallowed up by the giant storeroom. Instead there was the *tick-tick-tick* of scratching claws.

'Rats!' said Edie. 'Naz, they'll eat Impy!' Her hands felt clammy and cold as she thought of Impy trapped in a pipe as a huge grey rat with sharp teeth rushed towards her.

'It's all right,' said Naz, pointing upwards. A bark told them that the scratching claws were in fact dog paws racing across a concrete floor overhead.

'The others must be coming,' said Naz. They listened again, straining to hear, and there was another tiny *clink* in the distance.

'Along here!' said Naz, zig-zagging through more shelves. They turned a corner, breathing fast and running behind the tallest of the shelves, but as the nail clinked once again they found themselves back where they had started by Babar the elephant. Nid tumbled out of the pipe in an exhausted heap just where he had got in. There was no sign of Impy.

'Nid,' said Edie in dismay. 'You've just run in a giant circle!'

Nid, who rarely ever spoke, held his arms up at different angles to show Edie that there was a tangle of connected pipes. He hadn't known which one to follow. Naz picked him up and slipped him back in her rucksack where he sank into an exhausted sleep.

'She could be down any one of them,' said Edie. 'I'm such an idiot.'

'Or . . .' said Naz, trying to be positive, 'she could have found another way out! Maybe we should tell Fabien. He might be able to help us!'

'No!' said Edie.

A ball of snowy fur appeared, bouncing and yapping around their feet. It was Napoleon. He sniffed and snuffled at the rucksack with Nid inside, so much so that Naz lifted it up and cradled it to her chest. Sami came running round the corner.

'We heard you call through the pipes!' said Sami.

'Have you seen Impy?' said Edie in an urgent whisper, but Fabien arrived before Sami could answer. Sami sat on the floor beside Napoleon and he gave another curious sniff at her pocket.

'I know who can help you, Edie,' she said, pointing at Napoleon. 'Look! I think he can smell FLITS!' Then she immediately clapped her hand over her mouth. There was no mistaking what she had said, and no doubt that Fabien had heard it.

Chapter Eleven

Rue des Morillons

'Flits?' Fabien said, rolling the word around in his mouth as if it was an exciting new sweet. 'I like that word.' Then he bent down and rubbed Napoleon behind the ears. The dog had put his forelegs up on Sami's lap and was sniffing at her pocket again. 'Sami, what *is* in your pocket?'

'Don't!' said Edie, but Sami pulled the matchbox out of her pocket.

'I'm going to show him!' she said impulsively and stood up.

Edie felt her stomach coil into a tight ball as Sami slid the matchbox open and gently levered Pea out so she was standing on the shelf. Then she placed the last of the doughnut beside her.

Edie looked at Fabien. He was staring at Pea, who was dabbing her finger in the sugar crystals and completely ignoring her audience of four children and a dog. There was a long silence as they all watched Pea, and then Fabien lifted his hand and for an awful moment Edie thought he was about to bring it down on the shelf and squash Pea flat as if she was an insect.

'Fabien!' she shouted, and Nid's head poked out of the rucksack, but Fabien simply lowered his arm very gently and, holding out his little finger, he allowed Pea to wrap her arms around it.

'I thought it was probably a *volette*! Napoleon is never wrong. He helps me to know where they are, but he never hurts them.' He pulled out the two thimbles of dough that he had sneaked out of the bakery. 'I think I have something here that she might like.'

'*Volettes?*' said Edie in a voice barely above a whisper. 'So you have them here too.'

'Of course,' said Fabien. He caught sight of Nid as Napoleon had pushed his wet nose into Nid's face.

'Oh, there's another one! Two English flits!' Fabien said, and this time, when he smiled, Edie didn't think about his teeth. She knew that she must ask what they were all desperate to know.

'Are there flits living *here*?'

'We saw one on a bicycle!' said Sami. 'And Impy ran after it.'

'Impy's the only other flit we have with us and

she's missing,' Edie explained.

Fabien merely said, 'Come.' He led them back up to the small kitchen at the back of the building and along a corridor to the far end where there was a small cubbyhole room with a window.

'This is my office,' said Fabien. 'It's where I work when I come here to help my grandmother.'

Edie, Naz and Sami squeezed in beside him. A desk with a stool ran right along the wall and it was littered with brown wrapping paper and string, labels, scissors and tape. At the end there was a window that looked out into the backyard, and a shaft of milky sunlight streamed through it. Fabien picked up two small corks and set them up in a row in front of a wooden pencil box that lay on its side under the window.

'Please,' he said, indicating that Nid and Pea should sit there. Fabien slid back the lid of the pencil box as if it was a stage curtain and there inside was a small furnished room. Tiny copper pans, like the ones in the toy grocer's shop, hung from the ceiling over a table made from an old box of drawing pins and set with two gold-button plates. The walls were papered with jaunty French biscuit wrappers and a pillbox bed was covered with a red silk quilt stitched from a tie. The whole scene was lit by a small bulb attached to a battery. Pea jumped off her cork and ran inside.

'You have a flit camp too,' said Edie, leaning in for a better look as Pea folded herself up in the silk-tie quilt.

'I help to furnish it with things left in the Lost Property Office that no one has collected,' said Fabien. He picked up an old chess piece in the shape of a castle that he was making into a coat stand. 'I wasn't good at schoolwork, but I'm good with my hands.'

'But there's no one here,' Sami said.

Fabien picked up the scissors and tapped at the pipes running along the wall above the desk, making a sound louder and sharper than Nid's nail and one that echoed through the pipework. For a moment there was silence and then Edie heard a low-pitched hum that sounded like a lazy bee and out of the largest pipe there appeared a tiny motorbike with a figure in a bottle-top helmet and scarf bent over the handlebars. He shot along the pipe, slid down a ruler angled as a ramp and skidded to a halt on the desk in front of the English party.

'Meet Enzo!' said Fabien.

Pea let the quilt slip to the floor as she stared and Nid, standing up on the balls of his feet, tried to stop himself from touching the gleaming motorbike. Enzo turned off the engine, pushed the bike onto its stand and took off his helmet.

'*Bonjour,*' he said and performed a small bow.

Pea clapped her hands in delight.

'Do all French flits have motorcycles?' asked Sami.

'Not all!' said Enzo. 'Most have –' He hadn't finished his sentence before another figure flew out of the pipe, but this time on a bicycle. The figure pedalled furiously, turning the bike onto the ramp with a front-wheel spin before pulling up alongside Enzo.

'*Deux minutes et quatre secondes*,' she said in French, stopping once she saw the crowd of faces looking back at her.

'And this is Mousette,' said Fabien. 'Mousette is Enzo's daughter. These are the Paris Lost Property Office flits!'

'Flits?' said Mousette. She undid the bag that was strapped across her chest and propped her bike against the side of the pencil box. Now she was standing upright, Edie could see she wore trousers just below her knee that were fashioned out of scraps of blue leather and a red patterned silk shirt that looked as if it was cut from the same tie that made the quilt. Her hair was tucked into a red felt beret. She took it off and placed it playfully on Pea's head as Fabien introduced the delegation from England.

Edie stared at them. She wanted to laugh and cry at the same time. It was so thrilling to see flits here too, living and breathing in Paris, but anxiety gnawed at her stomach as there was still no sign of Impy.

'Mousette!' she said. 'Can you help us? We have lost one of our English flits.'

'Oh, yes,' said Mousette airily. 'Yes, I have seen her. The one who stole my baguette!'

'Yes! That's right,' 'Edie said, almost shouting with relief. 'She didn't mean to take anything, it was just –' she jumped straight to the point – 'do you know where she is?'

'I found her wandering in the pipes near the kitchen and gave her my old cycle,' said Mousette. She turned back to the pipes and, putting her fingers in her mouth, she gave a piercing whistle. They all stood in silence, listening. After a few minutes Mousette whistled again.

'That's strange,' she said. 'I thought she was just behind me.'

'Are there rats in the pipes?' Edie asked.

'There is one rat, yes, who lives here,' said Mousette. 'But –'

'What if he caught her?' Edie cut in.

'He's very old and lazy,' Enzo said.

'Impy is much slower than you!' said Edie. She knew that her voice had a note of panic in it. 'So the rat could have got her! Or maybe she's had an accident.'

'Let's see if Napoleon can help,' said Fabien, and lifting the dog up he carried him outside into the corridor by the pipework. It was lower down on the wall here and easier for a dog to reach.

Edie watched as Napoleon scurried back and forth, his nose to the pipes, and after a few minutes he began to bark and wag his tail furiously.

'I think something is coming,' she cried out.

The pipes leading into Fabien's cubby-hole office began to clank again and they could all hear a distant bell ringing. The bell grew louder and, as Edie and Fabien squeezed back into the office alongside Naz and Sami, a bicycle shot out of the pipe, slid down the ramp completely out of control and collided with Mousette and Enzo's kitchen table. A bucket of water tipped up and a copper pan clattered to the floor.

'Impy!' cried Edie.

Impy stood up, dusted herself down and shook out her wings. She was covered in muck from the pipe, with a smear of rust on her face, and her hair was tangled, but she looked ecstatic. Seeing Edie, she waved joyfully. All their disagreements seemed to be forgotten.

'Seven minutes and forty seconds!' she said. 'I fell off on a right-hand bend, but here I am!'

'You made it,' said Mousette. 'And now you can teach me to fly!'

Impy laughed and, lifting into the air, she did a neat loop-the-loop, landing on Edie's head.

'Hah! Papa, you see that? Some of those English flits have wings! How I would love wings!'

'You already fly on that bicyclette!' Enzo called over his shoulder as he walked into the kitchen and tidied up the mess caused by Impy's arrival. He put on an apron made from pillow ticking. 'We must bake for our guests. Fabien, the dough?'

So that was what the dough was for! Fabien handed over one of the two thimbles of dough he had taken from the patisserie and Enzo set about kneading it and rolling it out with half a toothpick. Mousette squeezed a segment of lemon into a jug and, after mixing it with water and sugar, offered each of the English flits a glass as Enzo folded the dough into tiny half-moon shapes and placed them on a tray.

'How do you bake them?' said Impy. At the Hillside Camp cooking was done outside over small fires built from broken match sticks. Enzo pointed at a metal box hoisted up on a copper pipe that ran under the window.

'That is our oven,' he said.

'It's attached to a hot water pipe that heats the building,' Fabien added. Edie stretched out her hand to touch it. 'Don't touch! It's *very* hot.'

The tray was pushed inside the oven and it wasn't long before the sweet vanilla scent of baking dough drifted around Fabien's cubby hole and Enzo was handing each of the English flits a buttery croissant.

'Mmmm!' said Pea, cramming hers in her mouth all in one go, while Nid ate his sitting astride Enzo's motorbike.

'I can take you for a ride, if you like,' said Enzo. Nid looked as if he might burst like a washing-up bubble with excitement. 'And you'd all be very welcome to stay with us.'

Nid and Impy nodded wildly, but Sami scooped Pea up into her hand.

'Not Pea,' she said. 'We can come and visit, Mr Enzo, but please can Pea stay with me?'

'Of course,' said Enzo.

'She can keep my hat,' Mousette said, looking at the red beret that was now wedged firmly on Pea's head.

In the distance they heard Napoleon barking and Madame Cloutier calling Fabien's name.

'Are there other flits?' Edie asked. She didn't want to go yet.

'Yes, many,' said Enzo. 'My family lives near here on a deserted railway line.'

'Like us!' said Impy. 'We live in an old wilderness station in London.'

Madame Cloutier called again.

'I'll take you there tomorrow,' said Fabien. 'After we have given Monsieur Rottier his glass dome back. You'll like Monsieur Rottier. Like I said, he's a proper artist.'

'Thanks for helping to find Impy,' Edie said as they turned to go. It came out a little grudgingly, but seeing Fabien with Enzo and Mousette had changed everything.

Chapter Twelve

Passage de Curiosité – La Maison de Verre

The shops that lined Passage de Curiosité were like a secret row of glass-fronted cupboards with each window display a tantalising glimpse of what was inside. In one window there were boxes of coloured buttons and threads, and in another a large wooden stand with umbrellas and canes splayed out into a fan of spiny fingers.

The passageway itself was a covered arcade with a glass roof and a tiled floor, and above each shop there was a sign that hung from a twirly wrought-iron arm. Victor Rottier's shop sign had a glass dome on it with a bird inside and *LA MAISON DE VERRE* printed underneath.

'The Glass House Man!' Edie said to Naz.

Fabien pushed open the door and a bell jangled overhead. The room was lined with dark wooden panels and cabinets filled with strange trinkets, and it had a strange smell of vanilla and sour fruit. Glass domes with miniature theatrical scenes inside stood on wooden plinths and the head of a moose with huge antlers hung on one wall. Edie stopped to look at one of the glass domes. Inside there was a painted wax windmill set on the top of a theatre. Edie spotted a stuffed mouse dressed in a silk coat standing in the doorway.

'See how clever he is?' said Fabien.

'It's amazing,' said Sami.

Naz nodded but said nothing, and Edie decided that she didn't like the stuffed mouse.

Clutching the bag with the glass house butterfly inside, Fabien stepped forward and called up the stairs.

'Monsieur Rottier?'

There was the sound of a chair scraping across the floorboards and heavy footsteps. Fabien raised his eyebrows and mimicked an elderly man walking across the floor. A pair of scaly, pointed black crocodile boots appeared through the banisters taking slow, precise steps down the stairs and gradually Monsieur Rottier revealed himself to them. He wore a leather apron and his fingers, as he clutched the banisters, were long and elegant. His hair stuck out like two grey bat wings on either side of his head and his eyes as he turned to look at them were icy blue.

'Ah, Fabien! *Avez-vous mon papillon?*'

Fabien held up the shopping bag. '*Oui, Monsieur.*' For the benefit of Edie, Naz and Sami he said, 'He asks if I have his butterfly.'

'I see you have brought English friends?' Monsieur Rottier said in English.

'Yes. They are visitors from London. They have come to see how we work at the Paris Lost Property Office.'

'How nice!'

'Hello!' said Sami enthusiastically.

Fabien introduced them all and Monsieur Rottier's eyes scanned over them like the X-ray machine at the Eurostar terminal. Then he snatched the bag from Fabien and, plunging his hand inside, he pulled out the butterfly glass dome wrapped in brown paper.

'Ah!' he said, pulling off the wrapping. 'You beauty!'

'How can he think it beautiful,' whispered Naz, 'when it's dead and pinned to a cork tree?'

'Well done, Fabien! I was making a delivery for a customer and I left it on a station bench at Bastille. So stupid of me. Please thank Madame Cloutier.'

'I will,' said Fabien.

Monsieur Rottier set the butterfly jar down, drew a cloth out of his apron pocket and started to polish the glass. Sami wandered over to the mantelpiece and was staring at another of the miniature scenes inside a glass dome. A table was set for tea with a tiny white-and-gold teapot and a china plate of cakes and biscuits. She could see macarons and pink sugared almonds that appeared to be coated with sugar snow.

'Look at this!' said Sami. 'Can I eat one of those tiny cakes?'

Victor turned round and smiled, but it was a strange, oily sort of smile.

'Well, I'm glad they are convincing, but no, you cannot eat them. The whole scene is made from painted wax. Beeswax. From the hives in a famous Paris park we call Jardin des Plantes. That's what I do, you see, I –'

'Are you a wizard?' Sami interrupted.

Victor gave a tinkly laugh. 'Not a wizard exactly. But as I was saying, I make little scenes inside these glass domes for my customers to collect, and some of them do say my scenes are quite "magical". Now, as none of you can eat my wax cakes, perhaps you would like one of these?'

He pulled a paper bag from his pocket and offered each of them a mouse made of creamy marzipan with a string tail. Sami took one and licked its ears, crinkling up her nose as she did so. Marzipan was a strange taste. Odd, but not unpleasant. Fabien and Naz took one each, but Edie shook her head.

''Squite nice,' Sami said, taking a nibble. 'Sweet, but nutty.'

'Would you like me to show your English friends around?' Victor asked Fabien.

'Yes, we'd like that!' said Sami, without waiting for Fabien to answer. Then she patted her pocket and for a moment Edie thought she was going to bring out Pea's matchbox. Edie shot her a warning look and Sami dropped her hand.

'Thank you, Mr Rott-ee-ay.'

'Oh, *please* call me Victor,' he went on.

'Thank you, Mr Victor,' Sami said in an annoyingly sweet voice. 'I'm Sami!'

Fabien introduced the others by name and Victor led the way upstairs where there was another row of display cabinets and stands and lines of drawers.

On the long worktable in the centre of the studio was a flock of tiny, brilliantly feathered birds caught at the second they were lifting into the air, as if they had just been spooked by a cat.

'Are they made of wax too?' said Edie.

'No. They are –' Victor coughed – 'or should I say *were* . . . real birds.'

Edie nudged Naz and made a face, but Naz didn't make a face back. Instead she whispered, 'I know it's horrible, but you can't help looking at them.'

'Have you seen this?' said Fabien, pointing at a perfect replica of the Eiffel Tower crafted out of paper. 'And it has exactly the right number of steps.'

'Oh, I'd like to see the Eiffel Tower,' said Naz, moving over to join him.

'What's in the drawers?' asked Sami.

Victor pulled one open. Inside were butterflies of iridescent blue and orange, and when he pulled open another there were beetles of all sizes with shiny metallic shells and a scorpion with its tail curled upwards. All were pinned in neat rows and perfectly preserved. Edie tried to work out if they were made of wax or if they were real.

'Why do you have all these things?' said Edie.

'As I said, it's what I do. I make little scenes,' said Victor.

The children all walked slowly down the passageway between the cabinets, pulling out cabinet drawers and staring at the glass-domed displays.

'Look at that!' said Sami, pointing at a snake in a jar of pickling fluid. They crowded around the jar, but Edie thought it was dreadful and, drifting away from the others, she walked to the end of Victor's studio where there was a heavy velvet curtain. As Edie lifted one side she felt a cold draught of air.

'No!' hissed Victor. He walked up to Edie surprisingly fast and grabbed the sleeve of her coat. Edie dropped the curtain as if it had scalded her and Victor let go. The others were still looking at the snake jar and hadn't seen what had happened, but Sami came running up behind Victor.

'What's through there?' said Sami.

Victor turned round and, recovering his smile, said, 'Your curiosity is to be admired, young Sami, but there is work under development in there.' He added with a flourish, 'It is to be a . . . surprise.'

'A surprise?' said Sami.

'Yes! And when it's ready, I might show *you* first!'

'Me? Before anyone else?' said Sami, her eyebrows arching up into her fringe.

'Well . . . it is something for *children,* so I would value your opinion.'

Edie could see Sami puffing up at this offer of a role as Victor's special advisor.

'I'd like that, Mr Victor . . . very much!'

Just at that moment, there was a sharp tap at the window by the stairs.

'Ah, Pigalle is here!' Victor said. He picked up a paper bag from his worktable and unlatched the window.

A large black crow stood on the sill.

Chapter Thirteen

Passage de Curiosité – La Maison de Verre

Kraaa! the crow said, flapping its wings and eyeing the paper bag greedily.

'Here, Sami! Come and feed Pigalle.'

Sami came to the window, holding out her palm, and Victor filled it with seed from the bag. The crow's beak darted across the sill and pecked at her hand.

'It tickles!'

Edie stared at Pigalle, at the way he cocked his head to one side, at the awkward tuft of bristly feathers on his beak. Could it be the same bird? Could it actually be *Shadwell*? Victor's sudden change in behaviour when she had opened the curtain had made her very uneasy.

Pigalle, absorbed with the seed, ignored her completely and, when he finished, he turned and shook out his tail feathers before flying off into the Parisian sky.

'Why is he called Pigalle?' she asked.

'Because Pigalle Metro station is where I found him,' said Victor. 'Such a tame bird. He comes to visit most days.'

'Do all crows have those bristles?' Sami asked, rubbing the top of her own nose as if it was a beak.

'Yes, of course,' said Victor. 'Look over here.' He led Edie and Sami to a large glass dome on the right of the stairs that Edie hadn't seen before. Inside were two stuffed crows on a perch. They stared back at her, one with its head cocked to one side and the other with its wings slightly opened, as if they had suddenly been disturbed. Their feathers gleamed and they looked so alive that Edie felt if she was to put her hand out with some seeds they would dart forward and peck at it.

'Do you see the bristles?' Victor said. Edie and Sami could see that both birds had a short fan of whiskery feathers around the base of their beak.

'Just like Pigalle,' he said, but the crows remained rigid and silent.

'Were they alive once?' said Sami.

'They were, but of course they were dead by the time I received them into my care!'

You mean, before you stuffed them! Edie thought to herself.

'Now, everyone, I think it's time to go back downstairs. I have work to do.'

Victor led the way, with Sami close behind, chattering happily about the birds in her garden being nowhere near as interesting as Pigalle.

'That crow reminded me of Shadwell,' Edie whispered to Naz, who had been looking through the drawers with Fabien. 'The crow I was telling you about at Wilde Street.'

'Don't all crows look the same?' Naz whispered back. 'And why would it ever fly this far?'

'I suppose you're right,' said Edie. Then she pulled Naz close to her. 'Victor got really cross with me when I tried to open that curtain at the end, and he grabbed my coat.'

'Did he hurt you?' whispered Naz.

'No, but it was a bit scary.'

'Maybe you were being too nosey,' said Naz, giggling. 'He's probably just grumpy. Aren't artists a bit precious about their work?'

'Maybe. It's a weird shop though, Naz,' Edie said.

'Yeah. It is! I didn't like the trapped butterfly, but I sort of quite liked seeing all the other spooky stuff. It's like Halloween. And you have to admire how he does it, don't you?' They could hear Sami chattering away with Victor at the bottom of the stairs.

'Better go down before she says too much,' said Naz and she hurried down after her.

At the top of the stairs, Edie paused to look back at the worktable. Alongside the flock of birds that Victor seemed to be working on, there were small jars of potions and preservatives, a pair of silver tweezers, a bag of wool stuffing, some small brushes, scissors and long spikes.

'He told me his brushes are made of camel hair,' Fabien said from behind her. He had stopped to take a last look at a shiny scarab beetle. 'I think it's the most exciting shop in Paris!' he went on.

I'm not sure I do, Edie thought to herself, but she nodded at Fabien and said nothing.

'Come along now, please!' Victor was standing at the bottom of the stairs looking up at them, his blue eyes like two searchlights.

'Coming!' said Fabien, clattering down after him.

Edie took one last look at the strange museum-like shop, her eyes roaming over the brushes and tweezers. Maybe Pigalle *was* just another crow like the two in the display. There must be hundreds of crows roaming about between here and London, all with bristly beaks and, as Naz said, this was a long way from Wilde Street.

Then she saw it and froze. A half-concealed eyeglass dangling from the wall behind Victor's desk. It looked almost exactly like the one Shadwell had snatched from Vera Creech. Pigalle was one thing, but this seemed too much of a coincidence. She wished Impy hadn't stayed at the Lost Property Office with Mousette as she needed to see this. She walked down the stairs in a daze.

'Can we come back tomorrow, Mr Victor?' Sami was asking.

'Why not!' said Victor. 'Come back in the morning . . . and I will show you my work in progress.'

Edie felt there was something very wrong about Monsieur Rottier and his shop, but she knew that this was not the time or the place to say anything. They were due to meet Dad at the waxwork museum in half an hour. Tomorrow she could get a closer look at the eyeglass.

Chapter Fourteen

Passage Delphine to **La Petite Ceinture**

The waxwork museum faced the main boulevard just off a neighbouring passageway called Passage Delphine. There was a doorway to the museum from the passage itself that would eventually take them to the workshops of the sculptor who was going to make a mould of Dad's face. The doorway looked like the entrance to a circus tent. It was painted a rich crimson and a hand with a golden finger pointed the way in.

They were greeted by Madame Cloutier.

'Come this way,' she said. 'Your papa is with Claude Epingler, the sculptor.' She led them through a series of museum halls, pointing out waxwork figures of famous French celebrities on the way.

'Here is the French Sun King, Louis XIV. And here is the artist Picasso. Over there the footballer Kylian Mbappé. And look, Edie, it is your Queen Elizabeth!'

They paused to admire the waxwork queen, who was wearing a green dress and a large hat decorated with roses.

Madame Cloutier took them up some winding stairs at the back of the museum to the sculptor's studio. Claude Epingler had a twist of salt-and-pepper hair curled up into a quiff and a tape measure dangling from around his neck. Dad was sitting in a large leather chair as Claude took measurements of his face with a pair of calipers and marked Dad's cheekbones, ears and nose with a series of felt-tip dots, carefully noting the distance between each. Claude looked slightly aghast when the gang of children trooped in, and when Dad tried to itch his nose Claude said in a pleading whine, 'Please, Monsieur Winter, you must stay still!'

Edie could only smile to herself that the famously squashy Winter nose (which she had too) was finally being set into clay and then wax, and she took a photo for Mum. Then she joined the others, who were sitting in a neat row on hard-backed chairs at the edge of the room. They sat watching for nearly an hour as Claude dotted and measured and calipered and his assistant took photographs. It was a slow and dull process.

Claude demanded utter quiet, issuing a sharp 'Sssshhh!' like steam from a kettle whenever anyone talked or so much as swung their legs against their chair.

Sami couldn't stop fidgeting and Fabien tapped his foot on the ground like a woodpecker. He rolled his eyes at Naz, which made Edie bristle as she knew he was still jealous of the attention Dad was getting for his waxwork.

'Can we go and see the other flits on the old railway line like you said?' Sami whispered to Fabien after Claude had given her a particularly sharp look.

Fabien jumped up. '*Mamie,* can we go? We have to walk Napoleon before it gets dark!'

'Ssshhhh!' hissed Claude.

'Yes, maybe it *is* time to go,' agreed Madame Cloutier. She offered to drive them back to the Lost Property Office in her yellow Citroën.

'See you later, Dad,' said Edie.

Dad carefully waved goodbye without moving a muscle in his face and Claude could barely disguise his relief as they all left.

'Farewell!' he cried joyfully.

With Fabien in the front and Naz, Edie and Sami in the back, Madame Cloutier drove at high speed, much like her grandson ran, as they left the passages behind them. She had her hand on the horn most of the way down the Champs-Élysées.

'*Stupide chauffeur!*' yelled Madame Cloutier as they circled around the Arc de Triomphe and Place du

Trocadéro and crossed the bridge over the River Seine. The air was damp and drizzly and a light mist had fallen as the Eiffel Tower loomed out of the fog.

'Look at that!' said Naz, her face pressed to the car window as they passed the Eiffel Tower. They had been so busy that they had almost forgotten they were tourists too. 'I've been longing to see it!'

The elegant iron girders swept upwards into an elongated pyramid, but the top was softened and smudged. It was as if someone had dipped Paris in fine powder and everything had turned a pale, pearly white. When they reached the Lost Property Office it was even foggier.

'Come on!' said Fabien, snatching Napoleon's lead from a peg on the wall.

In Fabien's office Enzo was giving Nid a motorcycle lesson and Impy and Mousette were having cycling races, but Enzo and Impy agreed to come with them, leaving Nid to polish the motorcycle and imagine that, for one afternoon at least, it was his own.

They jogged through a small network of streets to the west of the Lost Property Office with Napoleon running along beside them, until they reached a main road by some metal railings. The railings overlooked an old railway line that was now a public walkway with a sandy path running along the route of the old train tracks.

Large sections of the old railway had been turned into a park for Parisians so that it circled most of the city in a corridor of green. Steps led down to this section, which was in the 15th district of Paris.

'It used to carry passengers in steam trains before everyone took the Metro,' said Fabien as they stood by the railings. 'And it's called La Petite Ceinture.'

'What does that mean?' Naz asked.

'It means the "little belt",' said Fabien. 'Because it runs around almost all of Paris.'

Sensing that Fabien might be about to launch into a lecture about old train lines and stations, Edie quickly stepped in.

'Where is your family, Enzo?'

Enzo, who was sitting on Fabien's shoulder, pointed down the track.

'That way,' he said. 'We must walk for a few minutes.'

Tendrils of mist were snaking around their feet as they hurried down the staircase and onto the sandy pathway at the bottom. Behind them an old tunnel was boarded up and covered in tags of colourful graffiti. Fabien let Napoleon off the lead.

'It's like home!' Impy said as she flitted about overhead.

The track was elevated in places so that it crossed over busy roads below and they could see into the windows of apartments where families were already preparing supper and watching TV. Napoleon raced ahead, his white fur merging with the mist as he burrowed about in the undergrowth. A couple walked by with another dog on a lead and a carrier bag of vegetables and they passed a café that was once a station ticket office closing its shutters for the night.

After ten minutes or so, Napoleon shot into a particularly thick spot of undergrowth off to the left and Fabien led them through the brambles and shrubbery to a small clearing that couldn't easily be seen from the track. There was a pile of old wooden railway sleepers that had once formed the track bed for the railway lines.

'My home,' said Enzo proudly.

'Look!' said Sami, pointing to a broken flower pot that was home to a small cycle park and a tiny scooter-sized motorcycle like Enzo's.

'Do most French flits have bicycles and scooters?' Edie asked, remembering what they might or might not have seen in the Metro.

'Yes!' said Enzo. 'We might not have wings, but we are still fast.'

'Could we have seen some flits in a Metro station – the one at Bastille?' asked Naz.

'Yes, there is a camp of flits at Bastille who live in the Metro and they have a network of cycle lanes through the drains and gutters.'

'So they *were* flits!' Edie said to Impy.

Enzo, indicating that Impy should follow him, set off up a ladder to the top of the pile of sleepers. Edie could see the familiar signs of flit houses. Egg-box walls and biscuit packets created rooms furnished with tables and chairs from buttons and corks, matchboxes and empty pots of French jam. The roofs were strung with the mesh netting from bulbs of garlic and covered with leathery evergreen leaves. All these created a street of small houses for Enzo and Mousette's family.

Enzo introduced them one by one – his parents, his two sisters and his aunts, uncles and cousins. They all shook hands with Impy, marvelling at her wings, and they all laughed at Pea who ran up and down the ladder and in and out of the houses still wearing Mousette's red beret. A high-pitched bark alerted them to the fact that Napoleon had trotted on ahead and was some way up the track.

'I'll go,' said Edie, taking Napoleon's lead from Fabien. She had heard the gentle ting of her phone in her rucksack and hoped it was Mum. She walked out from behind the undergrowth and back onto the track, swiping through her texts as she walked. The light was beginning to go and everything looked soft at the edges as the fog had grown thicker. The Parisian apartment buildings were nothing more than grey shapes and the track they had walked along seemed to disappear into a ghostly nothingness. Edie felt the damp air in her hair and she pulled up her hood. She sent a quick message to Mum, only looking up when Napoleon barkcd again.

At the edge of the fog she could see the shadowy outline of a man. He was standing just off the track in among a patch of brambles and was holding a stick that he appeared to be sweeping back and forth through the bushes. Napoleon's barks were becoming more agitated and Edie could just see him bouncing around the man's feet. She wondered if it might be a park keeper, as the figure was wearing a long coat and there was a net at the end of his stick. But then he cursed and his foot kicked out at Napoleon – Edie knew a park keeper would never do something like that.

Edie started to run towards Napoleon, but as she got nearer she slowed down. She had recognised the bat-wing hair squashed under a hat and the scaly black crocodile boots.

It was Victor Rottier!

Chapter Fifteen

La Petite Ceinture

Victor swung round, catching sight of Edie. He appeared to be fiddling with his stick as he turned. The stick was a silver-topped cane like the ones Edie had seen in the shop window close to Victor's. She saw him quickly flip open the silver top and press it – the net was sucked back inside. In his other hand he was holding a wooden box. The veneer of oily charm that he had used in the shop had completely disappeared – he seemed angry.

'*Chien stupide!*' he said.

Edie bent down and grabbed hold of Napoleon's collar. The fur on the back of Napoleon's neck stood up like a comb, but he stopped barking and stood obediently by Edie, allowing her to clip on his lead. With Napoleon tethered, Victor recovered a little and brushed himself down. Edie pushed her hood back off her face and Victor's eyes narrowed.

'Ah!' he said. 'Well, this is a surprise. The English friend of Madame Cloutier's boy.'

'Sorry about the dog,' Edie said. She glanced back down the track and could just see Fabien and the others stepping out from the brambles.

'You should keep that dog under control. And might I ask what you are doing out here at this time?'

Edie felt she might ask Victor Rottier the exact same question.

'We were just taking Fabien's dog for a walk. The Lost Property Office isn't far from here and Fabien wanted to show us the old railway line.'

'Of course!' Victor had recovered his slick smile. 'It is famous in Paris.' Edie looked at the box he was holding in his other hand. It was wooden with small, drilled holes and a rope handle.

'Is your shop closed this afternoon?' asked Edie.

'I closed a little early,' said Victor.

'Do you live near here then?'

'No, I live in the north of Paris. This is a . . . field trip.' He finished abruptly without elaborating any further and he was clearly irritated by Edie's interrogation. She pointed at the bottom of his cane, firing questions at him like peas from a pea shooter, just as Sami might.

'What's your net for?'

'Butterflies!' Victor said, frowning. 'And this is my collecting box.' He held it up.

Edie felt confused. She hadn't seen a single butterfly and knew it was very unlikely there would be any on a foggy autumn day in late October. It was too damp and cold and it was nearly dark, but again Victor didn't elaborate. Instead he looked beyond Edie as Fabien, Naz and Sami ran up behind her.

'Ah! Here are your friends.'

'Monsieur Rottier?' said Fabien. 'What are you doing here?'

'Questions, questions!' said Victor, but before he had time to answer any more Sami ran past Edie and grabbed his hand, shaking it as if he was a long-lost friend.

'Mr Victor!'

'Hello, Sami!' Victor said.

'Can we still see you tomorrow?'

'Yes, of course. Would you still like to be my first audience?'

Sami gave a small, excited jump. 'Oh, yes, please!'

'Well, tomorrow then!' said Victor. 'I must be on my way. In future, young Fabien, keep that dog under control. *Bonne nuit!*'

He walked off back down the track the way he had come, swinging his cane and taking the flight of steps just beyond the café down to street level. The foggy blanket of grey swallowed him up.

'Look at that!' said Sami, pointing at something lying in the undergrowth. They looked down and saw a cream-coloured marzipan mouse with a string tail slowly dissolving in the rain. Impy and Enzo ran through the undergrowth to have a closer look.

'He must have dropped it!' said Naz.

Edie frowned. What was he really doing there? She didn't believe his butterfly story for a minute. 'Are there flits here, Enzo?'

'There's only our camp on this stretch of La Petite Ceinture,' said Enzo, 'but there is a cycle track we use close to the wall.' He pointed to the edge of the old railway line where the brickwork made a narrow roadway.

'What do you think he was doing here?' Edie said.

Fabien just shrugged his shoulders.

'He's a collector.'

'I think he was trying to hide something from me,' Edie said.

'Edie, you are always so suspicious,' said Fabien.

Naz shivered, pulling up her hood. 'Can we go now?' she asked.

'Come on!' said Fabien. 'It's getting dark. *Mamie* will be wondering where we are.' He set off at his trademark run back along the track.

'Isn't Mr Victor the most exciting person you've ever met?' said Sami as she jogged alongside Edie.

Edie said nothing. She did not think Victor was exciting. She thought he was very odd. Worse still, she had caught a glimpse of a chain that he was wearing around his neck under his coat that had sent more shock waves running through her.

Chapter Sixteen

Hotel Esmeralda to **Passage de Curiosité**

The next morning the fog lifted and Dad took them all for breakfast to a café close to the hotel. They sat looking across to Notre Dame with its bell towers and gargoyles sharply drawn against the blue sky and holding steaming bowls of hot chocolate and baguettes with French butter and apricot jam. Edie hadn't slept well, as she couldn't get the image of Victor Rottier walking off into the fog out of her mind, and when she finally dozed off she had dreamt of gigantic marzipan mice. She had persuaded Impy to leave the cycling races with Mousette and come back to the hotel with them the evening before, and as they ate breakfast she passed tiny morsels of bread and jam up to Impy's perch behind her ear.

'There's Fabien!' Sami said. She had spotted Fabien waiting for them outside the hotel.

Dad stood up. 'Right, I'll be off to the waxwork museum as you'll be all right with Fabien,' he said. He made a face at the thought of another day of moulding and measuring with Claude. They all laughed. 'Enjoy your visit to the Glass House Man!'

*

The bell above the shop door jangled as they trooped in. A woman walked out in the opposite direction carrying a parcel wrapped up in brown paper, and Victor was downstairs bent over an order book.

'Ah-ha! Here you are! Come along. Come along!' Victor said. He led the way upstairs where a row of stools had been set out in front of his desk. All the brushes and tweezers had been tidied away and there was no sign of the eyeglass anywhere. Instead, something large and oval-shaped sat on the desk with a cloth thrown over it.

'So, this is the first of three special glasshouses that I will be showing my customers on Friday,' said Victor. 'I am calling it La Grande Révélation, which I think you English might call "the Big Reveal".'

They sat on the stools and Victor adjusted the lighting so that there was one spotlight on the table. It was as if they were in a theatre. Under the cloth they could see a wooden plinth with a small silver handle.

'Sami, please come and wind it!'

Sami stood up and, with great importance, wound the handle until after several turns Victor pulled off the cloth. The glass dome was lit with a blue light and filled with a blizzard of small white  flakes twisting and turning like snow. It was like the snow dome Edie had been given as a child by her Finnish grandmother that you shook to create a Helsinki winter street scene. Sami turned the crank handle again, which sucked air into the dome causing the blizzard of flakes to become more vigorous.

'It's brilliant!' said Sami, hopping from one foot to another.

Even Edie was impressed. The flakes began to fall gently to the bottom of the glass dome and they could just make out a wintery Christmas scene. Against the painted backdrop of a mountain stood clusters of wooden houses around a square with a Christmas tree decorated with tiny fairy lights. Just to one side was a small frozen lake made of glass and right in the centre of the square there was a beautiful carousel. It had a red-and-white striped awning and glittered with silver and gold decoration. Painted reindeer on poles lifted up and down as it turned and music played. It was mesmerising, and Edie thought how much Mum would have loved it. As the falling snow thinned out figures began to emerge in brightly coloured hats and scarves, ice skating, and throwing snowballs and riding the reindeer on the merry-go-round.

Sami jumped up and down. 'Those people look so real.'

Victor looked pleased.

'It is my new line,' he said. 'This time I am creating scenes with people in them. It's very difficult work though, so I like to say that these are "expensive toys for expensive children".'

Edie knew exactly what that meant. Victor would demand a lot of money for his so-called toys.

'I am working on a circus scene too,' said Victor. 'I will display them in my window after the Big Reveal on Friday and crowds will flock to see them.'

Naz and Fabien clapped their hands as the theatrical spectacle somehow demanded, but Edie felt a bit sick. No one like her could afford something like this. She leaned forward to look more closely at the figures seated on the reindeer carousel and the skaters on the pond. She expected them to be made out of clay or plaster as the grocer in the toy shop at the Lost Property Office had been, but these creatures were extraordinarily detailed. As the snowflakes finally settled, Edie began to feel uneasy. You could almost see their eyes flicker, their muscles about to twitch.

Her fingers rested on the glass. She could feel Impy shifting in her pocket and she longed to bring her out and show her everything, but the creeping feeling of discomfort was growing stronger, winding its way up from her stomach to the roots of her hair. The music was no longer charming, but tinny and scary. She glanced across at Fabien. He was frowning and looking at the small figures too. Was he having the same thoughts? Were they real, living figures, frozen in position? Edie dared herself to ask the awful question. Were they actually flits?

Naz was staring at a small child throwing a snowball and then Edie saw her quizzical look turn to horror. Edie turned back and studied the figure of the child. This time she saw it too. The child blinked! Edie wondered if Fabien had seen it too, but Fabien was no longer frowning. Instead he was *smiling*! Couldn't he see it?

The shop bell jangled and Madame Cloutier's voice drifted up from downstairs.

'*Excusez-moi?* Fabien? Are you there? My car is parked by the museum and I can't start it. I need some help!' Fabien stood up.

'Don't go, Fabien,' she whispered.

'I won't be long,' he said breezily, heading for the stairs. Then over his shoulder he added, 'It's very clever, Monsieur Rottier. Everyone will love it.'

Edie was appalled. 'Everyone will *love* it?'

'*Merci*, Fabien,' Victor called after him and then he turned back to his remaining audience. 'Well, as I say, you are the first to see it.'

'Yes!' said Sami, excitedly bouncing up and down on her toes. 'The first!'

'Not everyone appreciates the magic of "miniature things",' Victor carried on.

'Oh, we do, Mr Victor! We love them too – just like you!' Sami said. And before Edie and Naz could stop her, Sami had plunged her hand into her pocket and opened up Pea's matchbox.

'Look at this, Pea! It's a magical snow scene with little people. And we're the *first* to see it!' Pea hopped onto the table and ran up to the plinth, scrambling up it to peer in at the glass.

Edie felt Impy peeping out of her pocket and heard her tiny gasp.

Then, even worse, Sami turned to Naz and Edie.

'Let's show it to Impy too!' she said carelessly. 'We've got two flits with us, Mr Victor. Oh, and another at the Lost Property Office with the French flits that live there, but he's learning to ride a motorbike.'

'Sami!' said Naz, leaning forward.

But it was too late. Victor Rottier had already pulled something out from around his neck. His eye was magnified into a giant, cold, glassy ball as he lifted the eyeglass and stared at Pea.

Chapter Seventeen

Passage de Curiosité

Naz swept Pea and the matchbox into her pocket and looked at Edie in horror as Victor slowly lowered his eyeglass. There was a furious tapping at the window and Pigalle's bristly beak appeared at the glass.

'Oh, let me feed him!' Sami said, not fully understanding what she had done.

'Well, of course, Sami!' Victor said, picking up the bag of seed from his desk. 'And perhaps your "small" friends would like to help?' He looked purposefully at Naz and Edie as he replaced the cloth over the glass snow dome.

'We don't know what you mean,' said Naz, who now had Pea safely in her pocket.

'Yes, we *do*,' said Sami.

'Can I feed Pigalle this time?' Edie said, trying to defuse the situation.

Victor handed her the bag and she filled her hand

with seeds. Pigalle cocked his head to one side and looked at her. He hopped from one claw to the other, then pecked away like a drill hammer. Now she had seen the eyeglass in full working order, she was convinced this was the Shadwell she knew from London. He paused and looked at her as if he too recognised something in her. Then greed got the better of him and he jabbed at her hand with his beak.

'He was very scrawny and thin when I found him,' said Victor, coming over and scratching Pigalle on the head with one long, tapered finger and with the horrible eyeglass dangling from his neck. 'So we must fatten him up.'

The shop bell rang downstairs.

'More customers!' said Victor, clapping his hands. 'The show is over for today.'

'Can we see the circus dome?' Sami asked.

'Maybe,' said Victor. 'Especially if I can see more of your "small" friends,' he added. Then he lifted his arm to indicate that they should all follow him downstairs.

Edie bent down quickly so that her head was alongside the crow's.

'You should be careful, Pigalle or Shadwell, or whoever you are,' she whispered. 'I think Victor only thinks of himself!' She pointed at the glass display with the two stuffed crows.

Kraaa! said Pigalle and he hopped back onto the windowsill but cocked his head and looked thoughtfully at the two stuffed birds.

Downstairs the shop had several new customers so Naz, Sami and Edie stepped outside into the covered passageway. A poster advertising Friday's La Grande Révélation was plastered across Victor's doorway behind them.

'You idiot!' Edie said angrily to Sami.

Sami looked nonplussed.

'She means . . . you shouldn't have said anything about the flits,' Naz said.

'Why not?' said Sami. 'I thought he might like to meet them. Can I have Pea back now?'

'Where is Pea?' asked Edie.

Naz patted her pocket. 'It's OK, I've got her. You were right about Victor, Edie.'

'Please can I have her back?' said Sami.

'Sami, don't you realise what you've done? Adults aren't supposed to *ever* see them,' Edie exploded. 'I wish we'd never taken you to the Hillside Camp and shown them to you. If it wasn't for you, Pea wouldn't even be here.' She scrunched her fists into a ball, barely able to look at Sami.

Sami began to cry. 'I'm s-s-sorry,' she said. 'I thought Victor was just being nice.'

'Edie, you're being quite harsh,' Naz said. Fat tears slid down Sami's cheeks, so Naz took her hand. 'There's a toyshop down there. We'll go and have a look round it for a bit.'

Edie nodded and watched them go. She needed time to think about what she had just seen. She moved further away from the shop window and opened the flap of her pocket.

'What should we do?' she asked Impy.

'He's using the eyeglass just like Vera Creech did in London,' Impy said, flying upwards and standing on the crook of Edie's elbow. 'You have to destroy it somehow.'

'And I think he's using flits in his scenes,' Edie said, turning her back to any passers-by.

Impy shivered, but she said, 'Why don't we go back inside and see if we can find out any more?'

'OK,' said Edie. 'But stay right out of sight.' She walked back to the shop, waiting until a woman who had been browsing downstairs left. She slipped back through the door without the shop bell ringing.

Victor was behind his order book and talking to a man in an expensive suit who was clutching a bank card. Beside the man stood a boy in a silk shirt and trousers that seemed very clean and pressed. She wanted to eavesdrop on their conversation, and Victor hadn't noticed her come back in, so she slipped down the row of cabinets out of Victor's eyeline and pretended to be fascinated by the beeswax tea party.

'What have you got this time, Rottier?' said the man, who sounded as if he was American.

'Something very special,' Victor was saying. 'I have arranged a special preview for you today, but there will of course be no sales until La Grande Révélation on Friday. Come this way.'

He led the way back upstairs and Edie quietly moved to the bottom of the steps so that she and Impy could hear what they were saying. There was the scraping sound of the stools being moved into position and the whirring of the crank handle winding up. The cloth must have been lifted as there was a loud 'Ooooh!' from the boy.

A few minutes later, as the snow started to settle, he said, 'Look, Pop! Look at all the tiny figures and LOOK at the carousel. Can I wind the snow up again? Let me do it!'

The crank handle clicked and whirred again.

'If you'd like to come back on Friday, I am presenting all three of my dioramas,' Victor said. 'And you will have first choice . . . if you secure it with a down payment now.'

The boy was talking excitedly. 'I must have one.'

'All right, all right!' the father said. 'What the boy wants, the boys gets!'

Then the conversation took a turn, which Edie was to think about for the rest of the afternoon.

'It's wonderful work, Rottier. So detailed. They could be real.'

Edie's mind spun. So the boy's father could see the figures too! She felt Impy tugging at the button on her pocket.

'Yes. Months of dedication and years of honing my expertise,' said Victor.

Edie could have choked on that.

'If you'd like to come back downstairs we can do the paperwork.'

'Pop! Did you see that?' cried the boy. 'One of them blinked!'

'Surely not,' said the father. 'Just super-clever modelling by Mr Rottier here.'

'It's full of surprises,' said Victor cryptically.

The tugging at Edie's pocket became more frantic and Impy suddenly whirred upwards alongside her ear.

'One of them blinked?' she said.

Edie nodded and gestured frantically for her to duck back down into her pocket and out of sight.

'When can I have it?' said the boy.

'Well, if your father makes a down payment now, you can have it on Friday afternoon,' said Victor. 'I just need it for my Big Reveal.'

As they crossed the floor upstairs, the shop doorbell rang again. This time a girl in a fitted coat with a velvet collar walked in. Victor's advance publicity was clearly working.

Edie slipped out of the door behind her before it closed. She stood outside, leaning against a wall and thinking fast. She was convinced now that the figures in the glass-house scenes were flits trapped inside some sort of casing, but she was confused as to how the boy's father had also seen them. Then it dawned on her that early on in the demonstration, Victor also hadn't needed the eyeglass to see them. He only used the eyeglass to see Pea.

'How can the father and Victor see them without the eyeglass?' she whispered to Impy. 'They're *adults*.'

'I don't know,' said Impy. 'He must be doing something with them to make them visible.'

Fabien appeared at her side with a patch of oil on his cheek from helping Madame Cloutier restart her car.

'Fabien,' Edie said, taking his arm and walking further down the passageway to an empty doorway where they could stand unnoticed. 'We have to go back to the shop alone tonight, to see if there are real flits in those glass domes. I saw one of them blink!'

Fabien looked both uneasy and unimpressed.

'Are you sure you didn't imagine that?' he said. 'Don't you think they could just be brilliant reproductions, made of clay or wax or something? He's well known in Paris for his birds and his butterflies.'

'*Real* birds and *real* butterflies, pinned and stuffed!' Edie cut across him quickly. 'His great new idea might be to use *real* miniature people like flits! It would be pretty easy, as he doesn't have to make them.'

'Would he really do that? The birds and butterflies were probably dead already and I don't think he'd use live flits,' Fabien said matter-of-factly.

'When I saw Victor down on the deserted railway line, he had a strange net,' Edie said. 'He hid it away before you came and told me he was looking for butterflies and that he was on a field trip. There are no butterflies at this time of year.'

'A field trip?' said Fabien. This was an English term he didn't know.

'You go on an outing to do research and collect things.'

'Well, maybe that was what he was doing, Edie? Collecting special winter butterflies or . . . I don't know . . . acorns for his miniature scenes. Anyway, adults can't see flits.'

'Some of them *can*,' said Edie.

Edie suddenly wished that Charlie was here in Paris with her. He would believe her! Or he would have done before he turned thirteen. Why was it so hard to convince Fabien?

Further down the Passage de Curiosité, the shop door opened and the boy and his father came out and slowly walked down the passageway past Edie and Fabien.

'On Friday, one of them will be mine!' the boy was saying, jigging up and down. 'I'm going to choose the winter scene so I can show it off at Christmastime.'

'I don't know how Rottier does it,' the father said. 'They don't even look like models, they're so realistic.' Their voices faded out of earshot.

'See what I mean?' said Edie. 'The man saw them too. If they are flits, Victor has done something that makes them visible to adults.'

Fabien's brow furrowed as he thought through the logic of what Edie had just said.

'If that boy's father could see them too, doesn't it just mean they're definitely *models*?' he said. 'And anyway, how would Victor catch them in the first place?'

Impy whirred upwards out of her hiding place right in front of Fabien's nose.

'Didn't you see Victor's eyeglass?' she said. 'That's how he sees us.'

'I didn't see any eyeglass,' said Fabien firmly. Edie wished that he hadn't gone off to help Madame Cloutier with her car just at that moment.

'Fabien, you must believe me that I saw one of

them blink!' said Edie. 'So did Naz, and that boy who just walked past, who is now hoping that his dad is going to pay loads of money so he can stick it in his bedroom.'

Fabien looked down and scuffed his shoe against the wall.

'I just don't think we should get involved.'

'What if it was Enzo and Mousette in there?' Impy said, fluttering right at the tip of Fabien's nose so that he had to cross his eyes to see her. 'Victor knows about Pea now as Sami showed her to him, and she told him that you had flits too at the Lost Property Office.'

'Sami shouldn't have done that!' said Fabien. For the first time he sounded shocked.

'Now will you come?' said Edie. 'Please, Fabien! I can't come back without you.'

Fabien looked thoughtfully at Edie and Impy.

'How will we get in?' he asked.

'I have a plan.'

Chapter Eighteen

Hotel Esmeralda to **Passage de Curiosité**

Sami had recovered from her outburst and was bouncing on her bed as if it was a trampoline.

'*Un, deux, trois,*' she cried with each bounce as the floorboards of the hotel creaked painfully and Naz tried to wrestle her into her pyjamas.

'Will you be OK?' said Edie, wondering if she should stay to help Naz.

'I'll be fine,' said Naz. 'We're going to call Mum in a while and then we're going to read this together.' She held up a battered copy of a Babar the elephant story that she'd found in the hotel lobby. 'It'll be like old times!' She looked at Edie and added, 'Be careful!'

On the bedside table, Impy was trying to settle Pea, who was running in circles around a teacup and counting along with Sami. She gave a resigned wave.

Two big sisters. Edie suddenly wished that she too had a noisy, impossible little sister to take care of and she felt bad, but she and Fabien needed to go alone. Now that Victor had seen Pea and knew about the flits, she couldn't risk putting Impy in danger until she knew what he was doing.

As Edie put on her coat, Sami jumped off the bed and stood in front of her. She took her hand.

'I'm sorry, Edie,' she said. 'I was stupid to show him Pea. I know the rule about adults and it's just . . .'

'You thought he might be a wizard?' said Edie.

'No! I just thought he was different, but I didn't like how he looked at Pea through his big eyeglass thing. I won't show him any of the flits ever again.'

'It's OK, Sami,' said Edie. 'I didn't mean everything that I said either.'

Dad knocked on the door and Edie walked with him down the twisting staircase to find Madame Cloutier and Fabien in the lobby.

Madame Cloutier was wearing a peacock-blue coat and a matching turban. She had invited Mr Winter to join her and her friends at a reception hosted by the mayor of Paris and to listen to his talk on the architecture of *la belle époque*. This apparently included a slide show of the entrances to some of the Parisian Metro stations.

Mr Winter looked awkward and out of place among Madame Cloutier and her friends, and Edie couldn't help giggling at Fabien, who was also standing in among them, uncomfortably holding two boxes of games, with his face scrubbed and his hair combed and parted to one side. The board games were the cover story for their plan.

'See you later, Edie,' Mr Winter said. 'We should be back around eleven. Don't do anything silly!'

Dad said this lightly. It was something he often said to Edie, mainly because he knew she *was* quite sensible. But tonight she was not going to be sensible at all. She was taking Fabien on a mission that involved leaving the hotel without anyone seeing them go, crossing Paris at night, breaking into a locked shop and making sure that whatever happened, they were back before Madame Cloutier and Dad returned.

Edie felt her shoulders tensing up under the weight of all this, but she smiled and said, 'We'll be fine, Dad. Have fun!'

The hotel had a small side room that looked out onto a square and in it there were two armchairs, a shelf of books and a table. Edie and Fabien settled themselves down and waved off Dad and Madame Cloutier through the window. Edie could tell from

Dad's face that he was wishing Mum or Benedict were there to accompany him.

'French Monopoly?' said Fabien, and then he added, 'Shall I explain the rules?'

'I know how to play,' said Edie firmly, but she did give Fabien a half-smile.

They played for about twenty minutes and then, when the receptionist was distracted by a large family party that needed to be checked in, they slipped out of the front door.

They took the Metro from Saint-Michel, changing once for the station at Grands Boulevards. It was a ten-minute walk from the Metro to Passage de Curiosité. The streets, normally busy with shoppers, were empty, and now the fog had lifted the skies were clear and cold. They passed bars and cafés filled with people and tried to blend in with families making their way home or heading out to the cinema.

Edie pulled her coat around her as they turned into the passageway. It was dimly lit and the signs hanging from each doorway were in shadow. A few pedestrians walked past as the passages provided short cuts between the grand boulevards and their footsteps echoed on the tiled floor.

Most of the shop windows were in darkness except for the toyshop, which was lit up to display a miniature Tour de France with a peloton of metal cyclists in brightly coloured shirts. They walked past the cane shop until they reached the door of La Maison de Verre. Victor had scrawled *Seulement deux jours*, which meant 'Only two days to go', in a red marker pen right across the poster advertising Friday's Big Reveal.

'Now what?' said Fabien as they stood outside the door. 'People will notice us if we try to break in.'

'We have to find the back entrance,' said Edie. 'The window sill where we fed Pigalle overlooks a yard.'

They walked right to the end of the passage and searched around for the entrance to an alleyway that might run along the back of the shops. Fabien found it: a wooden gate with peeling paint that was hidden behind some large municipal bins. It wasn't locked, but Fabien had to push hard to open it and ahead of them lay a long, cobbled walkway that ran down the back of the shops. It stank of old rubbish and damp earth, and smaller bins were dotted here and there like rotten teeth.

Each shop had a backyard that one or two of the more upmarket shop owners had transformed into a small garden with pots of geraniums and a metal table and chairs from which to take their coffee. They walked on until Edie stopped by a scrubby tree that had already lost half its leaves. The cobbles were cracked and broken around its roots, and its branches stretched upwards towards the thin sliver of light between the buildings. Edie had already spotted the familiar sash window with the wide sill.

'This is it,' said Edie. 'Victor's shop.'

Chapter Nineteen

Passage de Curiosité

The back door to the shop looked shabby and unused, and autumn leaves were piled up against it. Edie rattled the handle, knowing that it would be locked. Fabien looked up at the spindly branches of the tree with its skinny, slippery trunk and the distance between the closed window and where they were standing.

'Are you thinking that we should climb it?'

Edie didn't reply. She was busy looking along the line of the roof.

'*C'est dangereux*,' he said. 'We might fall, and the window is locked from the inside. Edie, is this really a good idea? What if we get caught?'

'Oh, we're not going to climb it ourselves!' said Edie. 'I've got another plan.'

She pulled a packet of sunflower seeds out of her coat pocket, which she'd bought for a couple of euros in the flower market on her way back to the hotel, and shook it hard so that the seeds rattled inside. For a few minutes nothing happened. Traffic hummed in the background and someone kicked some rubbish in a neighbouring alleyway and a can skittered along the cobbles.

'What are we waiting for?' said Fabien.

Edie shook the packet again and held a finger up to her lips. They stood in silence until a movement from the roofline above made Fabien jump. There was a flapping sound as if someone was shaking a square of thick fabric and a large bird landed at their feet.

Kraaa!

It was Pigalle. Edie bent down and held out her hand. The crow pecked at it greedily. Sunflower seeds were clearly a favourite.

Like Victor had done earlier, she stretched out her finger to rub the feathers on Pigalle's head. He backed away, looking at her suspiciously, but she smiled and spoke gently until he hopped forward, twisting his head under her finger for more caresses and eyeing the packet again. She noticed that one of his claws was slightly crooked as if he'd been in a fight or had caught it in a trap.

Edie closed the packet of seeds with a theatrical gesture and stood up.

Pigalle hopped about and pecked at her shoe, hoping for more. *Kraaa!*

She pointed up at a tiny square roof light set in among the tiles. She had noticed the dim shaft of light falling on Victor's desk earlier that day and looked upwards to see that the roof light was wedged open.

'You can have more if you fetch the spare keys that are hanging on the hook by Victor's desk.' She mimed shaking a ring of keys and turning one of them in a lock. Pigalle fluffed out his feathers and turned his back on them.

'Does he understand you?' said Fabien. 'And even if he does, why doesn't he speak French?'

'He understands enough,' said Edie, laughing. She also knew that whether he was in fact a Parisian bird or a Londoner, Pigalle (or Shadwell) was *not* a loyal bird. He just went where he saw the opportunities. She had seen that when he had abandoned Vera Creech at Wilde Street on the London Underground and flown off into the tunnel.

'You can have the whole bag,' said Edie, crouching down beside him, 'if you just get the keys.'

She shook the paper bag again and saw Pigalle looking at it out of the corner of his ringed eye. Edie pointed up to the roof light.

'It's easy, Pigalle. It'll only take you a couple of minutes.'

Pigalle gave a defiant *Kraaa!* but he stretched his wings and gave a small hop in an effort to take off in the confined space of the yard. After a couple of attempts he clumsily flew upwards into one of the topmost branches of the spindly tree. From there he flew further up onto the edge of the roof light and, tucking in his wings, he ducked under the frame and inside the building.

Edie and Fabien stood waiting for a few moments in silence.

'What time is it?' Edie asked.

'Eight-thirty,' Fabien said, checking his watch.

'So we have a couple of hours,' Edie said. 'Then we must head back.'

Fabien shifted his weight from one foot to another and glanced back down the alleyway. 'I don't like it here, Edie. Maybe we should go. I don't think you can trust that bird.'

'Just give it a bit longer,' Edie whispered, keeping her eyes fixed on the roof.

There was a slight clatter and a jingle of metal and Pigalle reappeared at the edge of the roof light, holding a ring of keys in his beak.

'See!' said Edie.

Pigalle flew down beside them and dropped the keys. In return Edie tipped more seeds on the ground and Pigalle hopped about pecking at it in greedy delight.

'I don't believe it!' said Fabien. 'That's amazing, Edie.' He looked at her with a new sense of admiration.

'Come on,' she said to Fabien. They went to the back door and worked their way around the ring of keys until they found the right one. The lock was sticky and unused as Victor must rarely use this door, but they managed to turn the key round and push open the door. It led into what appeared to be a kitchenette. There was a small sink with a tap and a hot plate with a coffee pot on it. Another curtain separated it from the main shop.

'We shouldn't turn on any shop lights,' whispered Fabien, 'in case anyone sees us from the passageway, but I've got a torch.'

Edie nodded and after fumbling in the cupboard under the sink she held up some matches and a candle. Fabien switched on his torch. Their faces were framed by the dim circle of light, their eyes wide, both as scared and excited as each other. Edie lit the candle and drew back the curtain to the main shop.

Chapter Twenty

Passage de Curiosité

The candle cast strange shadows around the walls as they tiptoed in between the racks of drawers and cabinets and the glass domes of stuffed birds and spooky miniature scenes. Everything appeared more alive now than it did in daylight and the moose on the wall seemed to watch them as they walked past, with its antlers casting shadows like two bony outstretched hands. Every stair seemed to creak as they walked up to Victor's studio and Edie thought of his scaly black crocodile boots making their way up and down them every day.

Fabien's torch flickered as he shone it around the studio and hovered over Victor's desk. The large glass snow dome had been moved and Victor's tools were laid out ready for the morning. Edie hung the spare keys back on their peg but only after slipping the back-door key off the ring and into her pocket. Victor was unlikely to notice it was missing and it could be useful. Then she walked over to the window and glanced out of it. She could still see Pigalle down in the yard eating the seeds.

Turning back to Fabien, she pointed to the curtain at the end of the studio that Victor had been so quick to protect. They pulled it back and walked into what looked like a storeroom. There was a workbench running along one wall with postcards of scenes pinned to a cork board above it and two spray cans. She leaned in to look at the postcards more closely. One was an Alpine mountain scene similar to the one Victor had already created in the glass dome and another was of a Parisian park with an ornamental pond and fountain. These must be the inspiration for his dioramas. At one end of the workbench there was a sewing machine with a basket of miniature clothes like dolls' house clothes – winter outfits with hats and scarves, a clown's costume and a beret.

'Flit clothes,' said Edie.

'I'm still not completely convinced,' said Fabien, frowning.

'But those figures in the glass dome – they were *too* realistic.'

'Where is that glass dome?' said Fabien. 'We have to find it. To prove that one or other of us is right.'

Edie pointed to the heavy metal door behind them. Fabien tugged it open and a blast of cold air blew across them as if someone had let in the winter night. This was what Edie had sensed earlier. It was a giant walk-in cold store.

The open door had triggered a blue light that lit up the inside so they could see that the cold store was lined with two shelves, but it didn't contain any food. Edie blew out her candle and they squeezed into the narrow space between the shelves. The blue light made their faces look pale and ghostly and they could see their breath.

On the shelves were three glass domes. The largest one was the mountain scene.

'It's here!' said Edie.

Fabien turned the crank handle and they watched as the snowflakes blew up once again into a Christmassy blizzard and the reindeer carousel slowly turned to the tinkly music. The second dome contained a circus tent with brightly painted scenery and a trapeze set up with three figures frozen into position. Two acrobats stood at the bottom of the wires and another was up in the air folded over a swinging trapeze. At the edge of the ring a clown was balanced on stilts.

The third dome was a Parisian park scene just as Edie had seen in the postcard. Groups of figures were arranged like families in the park, playing boules and hopscotch. A girl rode a bicycle, looking not that different to

Mousette, and a small boy was floating a model boat on the ornamental pond.

The cold was already nipping at their fingers and the tips of their noses, but Edie and Fabien stood and looked at all three glass domes. Each beautifully crafted. Each scene a miniature theatrical set, each figure dressed in a carefully stitched costume. Each one a small-scale world. If it wasn't so horrible, it would be magical. Edie could see that Fabien was beginning to think very differently.

'Do you think they're dead?' said Fabien.

'I-I don't know,' said Edie. 'We have to rescue them! We have to find out if they're still alive. Unfreeze them somehow.'

They stared again at the tiny figure folded over the trapeze in the circus scene and this time they both noticed the acrobat blink.

Fabien gasped and looked even paler in the ghostly blue light. '*C'est terrible!*' he said.

'What should we do?' said Edie.

'We can't just steal all the glass domes. He'd know straight away, and how would we carry them?' said Fabien.

'Why don't we just take one of the figures?' said Edie. 'He might not notice.'

The glass on the mountain scene was locked into place because of the complicated mechanism of the snow and the crank handle, but the circus dome was simpler and they were able to lift off the glass cover.

Edie slipped her fingers inside. She gently touched one of the acrobats standing at the bottom of the circus tent pole. He was cold and stiff, his legs rock hard like china. The whole figure was covered in a thick, transparent paint-like varnish and glued to the set. Edie tried to pick up the acrobat. She wiggled him to try to free him from the glue, but he was stuck fast and she was worried she might crack him in two if she tried any harder.

'I can't do it,' she said. 'Victor's stuck them all down!'

At that moment a red light started to flash and the cold store made a loud beeping sound.

'Quick,' said Fabien. 'It's because the door's open and the temperature's going up. We'll have to close the door and wait for the temperature to go down again.'

They eased the glass back over the top of the circus scene and closed the door of the cold store. Within seconds the red light stopped flashing. They stood outside, blowing on their hands and trying to get warm again, and as they did so they heard a tapping outside in the studio.

Edie peeped through to see where the sound was coming from. Pigalle was perched on the frame of the roof light and he was tapping the frame with his beak. When he saw her he ruffled his feathers and bobbed his head. Why was he behaving like that?

Then someone unlocked the front door and the shop bell tinkled downstairs.

Chapter
Twenty-one

Passage de Curiosité

E die whisked the curtain back across the doorway and blew out the candle. Fabien snapped off his torch, plunging them into darkness. Footsteps crossed the floor below them. Edie felt her breath quicken and she could hear Fabien nervously swallow. The storeroom was small and had few places to hide. In the dark Fabien took Edie's hand and quietly pulled her into the gap alongside the cold store. It was a tight squeeze, but they shuffled in beside it as far as they could and crouched down, listening to the quiet hum of the fridge beside them. They could also hear the stairs creaking as someone walked upstairs and crossed the studio floor.

'*Oiseau stupide!*' came a shout. It was Victor! '*Sors d'ici!*'

Victor's voice wasn't friendly at all. It sounded cold and malicious, but his French was clear enough for Edie to understand. He was talking to Pigalle.

'*Pas longtemps maintenant!*'

Edie wondered what Victor meant by 'not long now'. Something pinged off the glass of the roof light and with a flap of wings and a frightened squawk Pigalle was gone. The scraping of a chair across the floor and an angry slam told them that Victor had reached up and closed the roof light. The footsteps moved in their direction. Edie could now hardly breathe, and she willed her whole body to be still and silent.

The curtain was drawn back and, luckily for Fabien and Edie, its folds covered the gap between the cold store and the wall, hiding them from view, but Edie could just see Victor's coat through a tiny slit in the fabric.

The light went on and there was a clatter as Victor accidentally dropped something on the floor. It was the same stick that he carried with him on the deserted railway. Edie could see its silver top and the hinge that Victor could flip open to release or retrieve his net. He bent down and picked it up and in the other hand he held the wooden box with holes drilled in it and a rope handle. Edie recognised it straight away. He swung it up out of sight and with a clunk put it on the workbench. He switched on a radio somewhere and jazz music rose and fell as he pulled out a stool and bent over something on the workbench. He hummed along to the music as he worked and talked to himself.

'That's it. Just move that arm there and . . . adjust this a little. Not bad at all.'

Pssshhht! Pssshhht! There was the hiss of compressed liquid sprayed from a can that reminded Edie of Dad spraying his shoes before he polished them. Through the gap in the curtain, Edie then saw Victor hold up a brush and, over the music, she heard a sucking sound as if something was being dipped into a pot. The sound came several times and then the sewing machine whirred and clicked in time to the jazz music as Victor stitched something together. The minutes ticked past.

Edie could feel the pins and needles fizzing in her feet as her cramped limbs started to complain. She silently tapped Fabien's wrist. He pulled back his sleeve and the hands on his watch face shone a ghostly luminous green. It was nearly ten o'clock. Edie willed the watch hands to stand still. Whatever happened, they must get back to the hotel before Madame Cloutier and Dad returned.

Quite suddenly the radio clicked off and Victor stood up. He turned to the cold store and opened the door, and Fabien and Edie folded themselves back into the shadows as far as they could. They could hear him lifting and moving something inside it for several minutes. Then the door shut.

'There. All done!' Victor yawned. 'And that's enough for tonight.' He seemed to address someone else in the room. 'Your turn tomorrow!' But there was no reply.

Switching out the light, he walked through the archway and closed the curtain behind him. Edie and Fabien sat in the dark, waiting as he crossed the studio, walked down the stairs and out of the shop.

When they were certain he was gone, they crawled out from beside the cold store, rubbing and stretching their legs and arms to ease the pins and needles. They felt almost giddy with relief that Victor hadn't seen them.

The moon cast a silvery glow around the storeroom.

'Who was he talking to?' said Edie.

'I don't know,' Fabien said. 'Himself probably!' Fabien sounded cross. 'That stupid bird. You should never have trusted him. He must have alerted Victor.'

'But Victor lives somewhere in the north of Paris,' Edie said. 'Pigalle wouldn't have had enough time to alert him.' She didn't know why, but she was starting to trust the crow who flipped loyalties as easily as a pancake in a pan. 'I think he was trying to warn us that Victor was coming.'

'It's too much of a coincidence,' said Fabien.

'Didn't you hear how Victor spoke to him though? And he threw something at him. Anyway, Pigalle doesn't matter. What do we do about Victor?' said Edie.

Fabien looked again his watch. 'We should go,' he said. 'Let's think about what we do later.'

From inside the wooden box on the workbench came a thin sound like a sob. Fabien and Edie looked at each other and Fabien turned on his torch.

'That's the box he was carrying when I met him on the railway line,' Edie whispered.

This time Fabien didn't mention butterflies. The tiny voice spoke again and it was more distinct.

'*Aidez-nous. Aidez-nous, s'il vous plaît!* Please help us!'

Edie swiftly picked up the box and peeped through the drill holes. She couldn't see much, but what she saw struck a hammer blow. She placed the box back on the workbench and carefully slid open the front.

'Fabien, you have to see this!'

They both bent down and Fabien directed the beam of torchlight inside.

Fabien gasped. 'Edie, you were right!'

Huddled in the corner were two terrified French flits, one older than the other. One wore a cap stitched out of a scrap of leather and the other was dressed in trousers and a shirt cut from a Breton striped top. They looked dirty and ragged.

'Please don't hurt us,' said the smaller flit, his dusty face streaked with tears.

'We won't,' said Fabien. 'I promise.'

'Is he still here?' said the older flit. 'The man with the horrible fish-eye?'

'He's gone,' whispered Edie.

The flits seemed to relax a little at this news and unfolded themselves from the corner of the box.

'Do you have any water?' said the smaller one.

Edie took the thimble that was perched on top of the sewing machine and filled it from a jug left on the side. The two flits gulped it down. Whatever had happened to them had made them parched and thirsty.

'*Merci*,' said the older flit and introduced himself. 'I am Leon and this is my younger brother, Souris.'

'What happened to you?' asked Fabien.

'The man with the fish-eye hid a marzipan mouse in a drain close to our camp at Bastille.'

'A beautiful pink mouse with a string tail,' said Souris.

'We crept along the drain thinking maybe someone had dropped it or left it there by accident and we broke off small pieces, eating it . . .'

'It tasted SO good,' said Souris sadly.

'But that man was hiding nearby and he jumped out. The others ran away, but he caught us in his net.'

'And Violette, our sister, is missing. He took her out

of this box and we don't know where she is,' said Souris, and another tear slipped down his dusty cheek.

'Your sister?' said Edie. She looked around the workbench and along the floor, but she had a feeling of dread. On the workbench were scraps of glittery fabric like the acrobats had worn and some trousers like Mousette's and a jacket in Breton cotton stripes discarded on one side. A large spray can from the shelf lay next to them, the words POLAR FREEZE printed on the side in blue letters. Next to it was a pot of the transparent varnish and a tube of extra-strong glue.

Fabien and Edie looked at each other. So he was using freeze spray to lock the flits into position and to craft his hideous scenes and then he was varnishing them so they wouldn't ever move again. The giant cold store behind them was where he put the flits so that they stayed frozen until the varnish had hardened and set. It was pretty certain where Leon and Souris might find their sister, so Edie lowered her palm for the flits to step onto it.

'We think we know what might have happened to your sister,' she said. 'But you must be brave.'

Leon nodded and took hold of Souris' hand.

Fabien pulled open the door of the cold store and Edie carried the two brothers inside. The sickly blue light cast an eerie glow across their faces. Edie walked carefully between the two shelves and stopped in front of the glass dome with the circus scene. Leon hopped onto the shelf, dragging Souris after him.

'It's so cold,' said Souris, hopping from one foot to the other, his teeth already chattering. But Leon was staring at the circus. He started to bang on the glass wall.

'Violette! Violette!'

Edie and Fabien looked in and there beside the acrobat Edie had tried to pick up was a new figure. A juggler standing in the centre of the circus ring in a glittery silver suit, holding three beads in her hands as if she was about to juggle. She didn't respond to the banging on the glass. She didn't move at all. Violette was already frozen into position and the varnish was starting to set.

'Let's get her out,' said Edie, but as they tried to lift the glass dome off the plinth, this time it wouldn't move. Edie ran her fingers around the rim of the plinth, discovering a small keyhole.

'He's locked it,' said Edie. 'Like the other two.' She had also noticed the large blob of glue that stuck Violette to the circus ring set.

In the distance somewhere out in the alleyway they heard the clatter of a dustbin lid.

'We can't stay here,' said Fabien. 'In case he comes back. And Edie, we've only got half an hour to get back to the hotel before your dad and *Mamie*.'

Leon gave a strangled gasp. 'We can't leave Violette!

Why don't you break the glass? Or take the whole thing with you?' He hammered again on the glass wall. 'Vio-lette!'

'We can't,' Edie said. 'Not tonight anyway. If Victor finds the glass is smashed or the whole circus dome gone, he will know someone has been here. We can't let him know that if we are to save them all!'

'Well then, we are not coming with you. We are staying here,' said Leon.

'And end up like Violette?' said Edie. 'Stuck in a painted case as circus jugglers or acrobats. I heard him say that he would be back for you both tomorrow! If you come with us now we can make it look as if you accidentally escaped somehow.'

'She's right,' said Souris. 'At least if we escape, we can go back to Bastille and get help.'

Leon's shoulders slumped and he gave a tiny nod.

'We are going to help you too,' said Edie.

'I'm just going to get some samples of whatever it is Victor is using, and then we *must* all go,' Fabien said. 'If we're not back by eleven they'll send out a search party.'

He pulled a fish paste jar out of his bag and another thimble and quickly smeared some glue inside the thimble and let the varnish drip off the end of the paintbrush into the jar before shoving both back in his bag. They put the collecting box back where they had found it, but tipped it on its side with the door slightly open so that it looked as if it had fallen over. This would explain why the two brothers were no longer inside. There was a small vent in the wall behind the box and there were numerous gaps in the floorboards that they could have escaped through. Victor would be unlikely to suspect anything more.

Fabien opened his jacket and slipped the two flits into his pocket, then they crept across the studio using only the moonlight to guide them. They hurried down the stairs and out of the back door, locking it behind them with the key that Edie had taken from the ring. Then they started to run. It was only when they reached the end of the alleyway and were the other side of the painted gate that Fabien spoke.

'You were absolutely right, Edie, and I'm sorry I didn't believe you. Victor Rottier is no good, and we have to do something.'

Chapter Twenty-two

Hotel Esmeralda to **Passage de Curiosité**

'Faster,' Fabien said as their footsteps clattered through the deserted flower market.

It was five to eleven. They ran past the great towers of Notre Dame and across the bridge, expecting to see Dad and Madame Cloutier framed in the doorway of the hotel. How would they explain where they had been? But there was no one there. Fabien slowed to a walk and Edie clutched her side and tried to slow her breathing.

'They must be late,' she said.

The receptionist had been replaced by the night porter, who was asleep at his desk and only stirred slightly as they slipped into the side room. They resumed their board game, trying to look innocent, and Fabien sat Leon and Souris on the windowsill, giving them each a tiny square of chocolate.

'So what do we do now?' Edie whispered. 'Victor's Big Reveal is the day after tomorrow.'

They both looked at Leon and Souris.

'We'll have to go back to Victor's shop again tomorrow night and try to rescue all the imprisoned flits,' Fabien said.

Edie knew he was right, but the thought of returning to Victor's shop made her shudder. She knew Victor would be completely ruthless if they were caught, and Violette and the others might remain stuck in those glass domes forever.

'How will we free them and unstick the glue and all that strange varnish?'

'Let me take Leon and Souris home tonight,' said Fabien. 'They can stay with Enzo and Mousette. Enzo's brother knows everything about plants and herbal medicine. He might be able to help us with whatever it is Victor has covered them with.'

A taxi drew up outside the hotel and there was a chorus of voices as Madame Cloutier and two of her friends climbed out of the car with Dad.

'Ah! Still up, Edie!' said Dad, walking into the foyer. 'Sorry we're a bit late.'

'I stayed up to keep Fabien company,' Edie said,

relieved that she had managed to recover from their dash across Paris.

'Good for you!' Dad said. He was a little flushed from the mayor's lecture and the accompanying wine, and the laughter from the doorway proved that it had been a success.

'I learnt so much about the design of the Paris Metro and the building of the Eiffel Tower!' Dad said. 'How was your game?'

'It was good,' said Edie. 'And *I've* learnt so much about the streets of Paris.' But she didn't mean the streets and stations displayed on their Monopoly board. She meant the moonlight on the Grands Boulevards, the echoing footsteps in the Passage de Curiosité and the illuminated bridges she had seen as they ran back to the hotel from the Île de la Cité. That was a much more exciting way to discover a city.

Fabien left with Leon and Souris safely stowed in his bag and carrying the two board games. He was surrounded by Madame Cloutier's friends chattering and ruffling his hair. As he looked back, he made a face like a sour lemon, which made Edie laugh.

'See you tomorrow,' he said.

'And tomorrow is a day of sightseeing,' said Madame Cloutier. 'Claude now has all the measurements he needs for Monsieur Winter's waxwork.'

Fabien gave a small victory wave. They were at last becoming friends, but the thought of returning to Victor's shop once more at night was terrifying. At that moment rescuing all the trapped flits without being caught seemed like an impossible task.

Chapter Twenty-three

Eiffel Tower to Les Tuileries

First thing on Thursday morning, Madame Cloutier once again appeared at the hotel reception. She was back in her work blazer with no hint of the turquoise turban, but she was alone.

'Where's Fabien?' Edie asked.

'I have asked Fabien to run some errands for me this morning,' said Madame Cloutier. 'But he will meet us after lunch with Napoleon as he wants to show you a special park where you can walk the dog.'

Edie tried to hide her disappointment. She was impatient to see Leon and Souris again and to make plans with Fabien, and now she would have to wait until the afternoon.

But she had no time to dwell on this as the morning

was a whirlwind of Parisian landmarks. They rented bikes and cycled around the glass pyramid of the Louvre and ate coloured macarons from a shop on the Champs-Élysées. They climbed one leg of the Eiffel Tower, up to the first stage via the zig-zag of iron steps (all 328 of them, said Sami), and as they rose above the streets of Paris, they could see for miles.

'Isn't Paris brilliant!' said Naz for the hundredth time as they gazed over the grey leaded roofs and television aerials of the apartment blocks, over the boulevards and grand buildings and over the fountains and formal gardens that stretched right out to the skyline. Naz and Edie moved a little away from the others so that Edie could show Impy the view and they both agreed that it was lucky Nid was still staying with Enzo and Mousette, as he would probably have jumped off the railings and slid down the zig-zag iron girders all the way to the bottom.

Mr Winter took ninety-seven photos on his phone to show Mum when they got home and, for that morning at least, Edie didn't have time to think about what they had to do that night.

It was warm enough to have an early lunch sitting on green metal chairs by one of the round ponds in the Jardin des Tuileries. They ate filled baguettes and watched the breeze propel model boats with pastel canvas sails across the water, which you could rent from a small cart at one side.

Sami was perched on the stone lip of the pond, trailing her fingers in the water, and this time no one saw her do her usual act of showing Pea the sights of Paris. She suddenly jumped up and pulled at Naz's coat.

'Naz!' she sobbed as she pointed to a boat that was halfway across the pond. 'Pea's on board!'

Edie jumped up as Naz tried to reassure Sami.

'Is everything all right?' said Madame Cloutier, who was at the far end of the line of chairs.

'Fine!' said Edie, but she ran around to the other side of the pond as fast as she could, watching the model boat like a hawk as a gust of wind filled the sails and it picked up speed.

Impy flew alongside her, watching Pea's bright red beret and ready to perform an air–sea rescue if Pea got into trouble. Within minutes the boat had clattered into the side of the pond unceremoniously, with Pea clinging to the mainstay and looking utterly thrilled with her latest adventure. Edie was there to catch it.

'Wooohooo!' Pea cried, her hair blown into tufts around her lopsided beret. 'Again! Again!' she said as Impy climbed on board and ordered Pea back onto dry land. Edie picked her up and slipped her into her pocket just before the boat's owner arrived to retrieve his model.

'Sami!' said Edie, returning Pea to her. 'How many times have I said? You've got to keep her hidden away. No more showing her the sights.'

'I'm trying,' said Sami in a small voice.

As they resumed eating their baguettes, the familiar figure of Fabien appeared, jogging through the park with Napoleon. It was still only just after midday so Edie felt relieved that they had the whole afternoon to make plans.

Madame Cloutier stood up as Fabien drew level with them.

'This afternoon Fabien is going to take you to Jardin des Plantes and Mr Winter and I shall have coffee and plum clafoutis.' She pointed to a boring-looking café near the Louvre. 'And then we must return to the Lost

Property Office, as I have a visitor. Fabien, make sure you are back at Rue des Morillons by six o'clock.'

Dad looked as if he might prefer a walk in the park with Napoleon than plum clafoutis with Madame Cloutier, but he followed meekly behind.

Chapter
Twenty-four

Jardin des Plantes

'Where are Leon and Souris?' asked Edie as soon as they had left the Tuileries. Fabien lifted up his cap and there they were, sitting cross-legged on his head. He introduced them to Impy and Pea.

'We'll take them back to their camp at Bastille, but we told Enzo about Violette and he said we must go and see his brother, Albert – the one I told you about who knows about plants. I think he can help us find a way of unsticking the glue and the varnish.'

'We all know Albert Dubois!' said Leon to Fabien. 'We call him Albert the Apothecary! He is well known to Parisian flits for treating us when we are sick or hurt.'

They crossed a bridge and walked through the streets, keeping the River Seine to their left until they reached the iron railings of Jardin des Plantes. A grand entrance opened up onto a wide central avenue with sandy pathways, perfectly trimmed hedges and trees in neat rows. A small zoo filled the area of the gardens closest to the river and the huge cream-coloured building of the Museum of Natural History stood at one end of the avenue.

'This way,' Fabien said, letting Napoleon off the lead and walking to the right of the gates. He led them to a corner of the gardens that had been left to grow untamed as a patch of wilderness.

There were several birdfeeders hanging from the trees and the whole area was fenced off so that no one could trample across it. Right by the fence there was a large wooden insect house like the 'bug hotel' that stood in the corner of Sami's primary school.

It looked like a cross-section of a house with the front taken off so that you could see into the different floors and rooms. On the top floor, hollow sticks of bamboo were laid side by side to create nests for solitary bees and on the floor below there were clusters of pine cones and sawn logs with holes drilled into them for beetles.

The ground floor of the bug hotel was hidden behind clumps of shrubbery and close to the fence so, if they crouched down behind the bushes, they could almost put their fingers through the railings to touch it out of the sight of passers-by.

Fabien pulled back the leaves to reveal a shop that looked very much like a French pharmacy, complete with a green first-aid sign hanging on the wall. There was a ladder leading up to it and a long ramp, and a motorcycle, not dissimilar to Enzo's, was parked by it. The shelves of the shop were lined with jars and pots, and the floor was covered with baskets of dried flower heads. At the counter stood Enzo's brother, Albert. He was a slightly plumper and more serious version of Enzo, with the same grizzled hair but no jaunty scarf. Instead, he wore round glasses and a green lab coat that made him look a little like a grasshopper. He was grinding up something in a pestle and mortar.

'This is Albert the Apothecary!' said Fabien.

'Hello, Monsieur Dubois!' cried Leon from where he was now perched on Fabien's cap.

Edie set Impy down in his shop and she very formally shook his hand.

At that moment, a bee buzzed in with a sprig of evergreen leaves between its legs. Impy covered her head and shot behind a basket as it came in to land. To Albert and Impy, the bee was almost the size of a Shetland pony with a sting like a spear. The bee made its delivery and buzzed off again. Impy peered round the side of the basket, a dried flower stalk caught in her hair.

'Nothing to worry about!' said Albert, chuckling. His laugh sounded like the wheeze of a tiny set of bagpipes. 'The bees are my assistants. They won't hurt you. Jardin des Plantes is my laboratory,' he added. 'Garlic, camomile, feverfew and rosemary. Even weeds have their place. It's a natural store of tinctures and medicinal herbs. Plants give us everything we need.'

'Like how dock leaves help nettle stings?' said Sami, her hand curled protectively around Pea, who was still in her pocket.

'Exactly,' said Albert.

Fabien told Albert what had happened to Violette and described in detail what he and Edie had seen in Victor's studio. He also gave him the fish paste jar with the varnish inside and the thimble filled with glue. Albert adjusted his spectacles and took a sample of both the varnish and the glue with a tiny spoon. He placed each in a glass Petri dish and dripped various liquids onto them from his store cupboards. Impy stood at the end of his laboratory table, watching.

'The glue is quite simple to unstick,' he said after several minutes of experimentation. 'But the "paint" Victor Rottier is using is a little more complicated. It is mixed with a strange enamel. No doubt he wanted a shiny, transparent finish like a shell. We need to make a natural solvent to dissolve it for these poor flits.'

Albert pulled a book off his shelf and ran his finger down the index.

'Maybe safflower oil? Lemon peel. Some nettle,' he said to himself as he thumbed through the sections of his plant encyclopedia. 'Rose for glycerin. Vinegar, of course. Fabien, we will need a bottle of vinegar and some baking soda. A little rosemary. Crushed garlic?

Maybe not. But tea tree could be good. And we need sugar, water and yeast to make surgical spirit and some ethanol.'

'Mum uses tea tree as an antiseptic,' said Naz. Edie could see that she was carefully noting all that Albert said with the same concentrated attention she gave to chemistry lessons at school.

'Do you think you can free my sister Violette, Monsieur Albert?' Leon asked.

'You must give me a little time. And I can't promise anything! But I will prepare some poultices and a mixture for a dipping bath and return with you tonight to Rottier's shop. Wait just one minute, please . . .'

He frowned and pushed the Petri dish with the enamel varnish under a microscope.

'There is something very strange about this substance,' he said. 'It seems to be reflective and see-through at the same time. I've never seen anything like it before.'

Impy told Albert about how the enamel varnish seemed to make the flits visible to adults, and she repeated the conversation she and Edie had overheard with one of Victor's wealthy customers.

'You mean that adults can see Violette?' asked Souris.

'Yes, I think so,' said Impy. 'I think that's what Victor's doing. Once he coats the flits with the enamel varnish, then *everyone* can see them!'

The French flits, Albert included, stared at her in horror.

'That's why he's using them for his glass dome displays,' said Edie.

'Do you think the varnish being reflective has anything to do with it?' Naz asked.

'Maybe,' Albert said. 'But I have to ask: how does Victor Rottier see them in the first place to catch them?'

'He has a special eyeglass,' said Impy.

'And it might have come all the way from London!' Edie added.

'Then we must work fast,' said Albert. 'And you must destroy the eyeglass at the first opportunity.'

Chapter Twenty-five

Bastille and La Promenade Plantée

Within a few minutes of leaving Jardin des Plantes they had crossed the River Seine and were walking towards Bastille. Traffic circled noisily around Place de la Bastille and Fabien kept Napoleon on a tight lead. Naz looked up at the huge column in the centre, topped by the statue of a golden winged figure carrying a torch.

'What's that?' she asked.

'We call it the Génie de la Liberté, which means "the Spirit of Freedom",' said Fabien. 'It's a symbol of the French Revolution, which began here at Bastille and we celebrate every year with a national holiday. *Mamie* closes the Lost Property Office and takes me to the parade!'

They walked into the Metro and up the stairs to the open-air platforms where the French Revolution murals were. A train had just left and they were alone on the platform.

Leon took them down to the far end, close to where they had seen a glimpse of the flits before. The gutter at the edge of the platform was like an open drain and it ran the length of the platform and along the walls of the main ticket hall. From there, Leon explained, it connected to a whole network of drains and gutters that ran under Paris. The station drain alone was the perfect cycle track, Edie thought, as it was deep and smooth with high walls, and it slipped in and out of tunnels as it ran under steps and pillars. They had to be careful to avoid it when it rained and water gushed off the platforms, Leon said, but for most of the time the drains were secret places that belonged to the flits to use as they pleased.

Leon jumped down with Souris and, where the drain disappeared into a tunnel, they ran inside and then reappeared pushing two bicycles. The wheels were no bigger than a Polo mint and the pedals were the size of Edie's fingernail. Leon turned and whistled and within minutes he was joined by several other flit cyclists who shot out of the tunnel and jumped from their bicycles to hug both Leon and Souris.

'We thought we had lost you!' one cried, and then he cowered when he looked up and saw the four children and a dog staring down at them.

'It's OK!' said Leon. 'These are our friends and they are going to help us.'

'But where is Violette?' another asked.

The story tumbled out of Leon, how the man with the fish-eye had lured them out of the drain with a marzipan mouse. When he got to the part about Violette he started to cry. Souris patted him on the shoulder.

'Tonight we must all go together to the man's shop,' he said. 'There are many flits that need rescuing. It's not just Violette.'

'What about the rats?' shouted one of the older flits.

'We must have courage,' Leon said. 'And fight against Victor Rottier!'

'The mice will help us,' said another. 'And we have friends in the Metro station at Arts et Métiers.'

'The submarine station!' said Naz.

'They know all the short cuts around the Grands Boulevards,' said a third. 'There's one that comes up under the waxwork museum.'

'That's right beside Passage de Curiosité,' said Edie.

'Are you sure you'll be all right?' asked Fabien.

'Yes!' said a chorus of voices. Even the oldest of the cyclists raised his fist into the air.

'We will leave when it gets dark,' said Leon and, turning to Fabien and Edie, he added, 'it's a long journey, but we should be there by ten p.m.'

Chapter
Twenty-six

La Promenade Plantée

Edie gnawed anxiously on her thumbnail as they stood outside the Metro station and Fabien hopped from one foot to another. There were still a couple of hours before Madame Cloutier and Dad were expecting to see them back at the Lost Property Office, and several more before they could be sure that Victor's shop would be closed for the night.

'Let's go to La Promenade Plantée!' Fabien said suddenly, pointing to the opera house on the far side of the busy roundabout. 'It's another abandoned railway line that's been made into a park. The entrance is just over there behind the opera house. Napoleon can have another run.'

They climbed up some steps to the entrance as the

first part of the park was set on a viaduct that ran high over the streets of Paris. It was smarter and more formal than La Petite Ceinture (where Enzo's family lived) and had been landscaped into neat pathways around raised flower beds and rectangular pools of water. They wandered through, enjoying the late autumn sunshine and watching Napoleon racing around the beds and sniffing. Joggers and cyclists passed them by, as well as families with small dogs in smart coats. The park was a good distraction.

After a while the walkway sloped downwards to street level where the track ran between high banks and through a series of tunnels. The first of the brick tunnels was dimly lit and vines of trailing ivy hung down from each end. Their footsteps clattered around the hard walls and their voices were amplified and echoey.

'Hell-loo!' said Sami, and as it repeated itself back at her she said it again a little more loudly. Putting her hand in her pocket, she lifted up Pea and put her on her head just as Fabien had done with Leon and Souris.

'Look, Pea! A real Parisian tunnel.'

Pea sat cross-legged, hanging onto clumps of Sami's hair as they walked on, and for once Edie didn't worry.

'Can you teach us a French song?' Sami asked Fabien. 'Like a nursery rhyme?'

'Well, OK,' said Fabien, stopping. He thought for a moment and then sang the first line of '*Sur le pont d'Avignon*'.

'Saw la ponn d'Avigg-non,' sang Sami in a crude attempt at French. Everyone laughed so she sang it again, more loudly this time, and it reverberated off the walls. Napoleon's usually upright tail sagged downwards at the noise.

'What was that?' said Naz suddenly. 'Something swept past my head.'

'Ugh! Me too,' said Edie as something light and airy caught her hair like a finger of breeze.

As they looked around them, three little shapes flitted about and were silhouetted by the mouth of the tunnel. Light as air and silent as ghosts.

'It's bats!' said Fabien. 'They should be hibernating at this time of year, but maybe our singing has upset them.'

Suddenly Sami's hand was up on her head and her fingers fumbled back and forth across her hair.

'Pea?' she said, and then more urgently, 'Pea, where are you?'

Naz immediately crouched down to see if Pea had fallen off onto the ground and Edie shook out Sami's hood and the back of her coat.

'I just felt one sweep past my ear,' Fabien said, and he looked upwards into the arches of brickwork and the shadowy ridges of the iron girders that supported the roadway overhead. There were endless nooks and crannies up there.

'Do you think a bat has got Pea?'

'A bat?' said Sami, and she began to sob.

The four children looked up into the iron girders, but it was difficult to see into the shadowy corners, even when Fabien shone his torch. Impy flew up out of Edie's pocket and began to circle around.

'Will the b-b-bat eat Pea?' Sami managed to wobble out.

'I don't know,' said Fabien. 'Don't they just eat tiny insects?'

'But Pea is tiny and she could be mistaken for an insect!' Sami said.

'Maybe Napoleon can help us,' Naz said.

Napoleon ran back and forth, sniffing the ground with his tail pointed upwards like a radar. He ran along the wall and finally stopped, pawing at the brickwork and looking upwards.

'I'm going to find her,' said Impy, and she flew upwards above Napoleon, getting smaller and smaller until she reached the line of bricks at the seam of the wall.

'Be careful, Impy!' Edie called after her. She could just see the dark silhouettes of the bats swooping around Impy's head as she tried to scramble along the ridge towards one of the iron girders. For a moment she disappeared and Edie instinctively cupped her hands and held them out in case Impy had fallen. Several minutes passed and then a tiny figure reappeared below the bats in an unsteady line of flight. She landed on Edie's hand. Her hair was tangled and her face was smudged with brick dust. She took a moment to catch her breath.

'I can see Pea's red beret up there in the corner of one of those girders. It looks like she's sitting in an old bird's nest, but the bats keep flying back and forth in front of it. I'll try again.'

Once again she flew upwards over the heads of the four children standing below. Edie strained to keep her eyes on her until she was once again at the top of the brick wall.

Kraaa! The croaky sound reverberated at the edge of the tunnel. Edie turned round. A crow was sitting on the pathway at the entrance to the tunnel and its head was cocked on one side.

'Pigalle?' she said, breaking away from the others and walking towards it. 'Is that you?'

The bird hopped in a lolloping walk towards her and she felt in her pockets for rogue seeds that had slipped out of the packet. She bent down and held them out and saw the bird's one crooked claw.

'Pigalle, it *is* you!'

A ringed eye watched her thoughtfully before pecking at the seeds. She put out her finger and caressed his head. Then Pigalle did something very unusual. He flew up and perched on Edie's shoulder. It was almost, she thought, as if once again he was trying to tell her something.

'Edie?' Fabien was calling to her.

Impy had returned from another flight up in among the bats. She looked exhausted.

'I can still see Pea,' she gasped. 'But they won't let me in. They zoom about and their wings are too much for me.'

Fabien caught sight of Pigalle sitting on Edie's shoulder.

'It's not that bird again, is it? The same one that we saw at Victor's,' he said, amazed.

'Pigalle!' said Sami and she pulled out the remains of her lunchtime baguette. 'You have to help us,' she said, pointing upwards with one hand and giving him small pieces of cheese with the other. 'Pea's been taken by a bat.'

Chapter Twenty-seven

La Promenade Plantée

'Can you fly up there and help Impy get Pea back?' Edie asked.

Pigalle jumped down onto Edie's hand and cocked his head to look up into the tunnel. Very gently Edie slipped Impy between his wings and Naz took a hair tie from her hair and put it around Pigalle's neck.

'You can hang onto that, Impy.'

Pigalle flapped his wings and flew upwards with Impy hanging on tight to the hair tie. They perched up on one of the topmost bricks beside the iron girders.

Kraaa! said Pigalle loudly. As he did so the bats scattered, flitting about with high-pitched squeaks of alarm. Craning her neck backwards, Edie could just see Pea's tiny red beret in a crevice.

'I can see her too, Impy!' she cried. With Pigalle keeping the bats at bay, Impy was able to scramble along the pointing onto a girder and reach Pea. Edie held her breath as she saw Impy's arm, no bigger than a matchstick, stretch out towards Pea.

'Go on, Pigalle!' shouted Sami.

The bird left his perch and, sweeping back and forth, he flapped his wings at the bats like a great protective cloak.

Impy took Pea's hand and helped her out of her hiding place and back along the brickwork. Pigalle returned to his perch and they climbed up onto his back.

'Well done!' Naz and Edie called out as Pigalle took off again and with a long, arcing sweep turned towards them like a plane coming into land, but at the last minute, instead of dropping at their feet, he swooped over their heads and out of the tunnel.

There was a stunned silence as the four children stared after him, and then a long, drawn-out wail from Sami. 'Nooooo!'

Fabien was the first to speak. 'I told you we couldn't trust him, Edie.'

Edie said nothing. She couldn't believe that she had been so stupid as to misjudge Pigalle. Her elation at the rescue turned to fear. Where was he taking the flits? It wouldn't take him long to fly to Victor's shop and then . . . !

She didn't want to think about what might happen next so she took a deep breath. In spite of everything, she still had the feeling that Pigalle was on their side.

There was an explosion of frantic barking and Napoleon shot back down the track.

'I don't believe it!' said Fabien.

Victor Rottier was standing in the mouth of the tunnel. Napoleon had taken hold of the hem of his coat and was shaking it wildly.

'Get off, you nasty little dog! Get OFF!'

The coat tore as Napoleon pulled backwards. Once again Victor aimed a kick at Napoleon and the dog pulled harder.

Fabien ran ahead and grabbed Napoleon, lifting him up under his arm. 'Calm down, boy!'

'Don't say anything about the flits!' whispered Naz as she took Sami's hand, and the three of them rushed up to join Fabien. The urgency of her voice silenced Sami.

'That dog has no manners! You should control it,' Victor said.

'I'm sorry about your coat,' said Fabien flatly and Napoleon continued to growl under his breath like distant thunder. Fabien bent down to inspect the rip in the coat, but Victor pulled away, wrapping the folds of his coat more tightly around himself.

'It's nothing,' he said, and seemed to recover himself very quickly. 'Apart from your dog . . . this is a nice surprise,' he said in a syrupy voice. 'Madame Cloutier did mention that you might be on La Promenade Plantée.'

Madame Cloutier? When did he see *her*? Edie could tell that Fabien was thinking the same thing.

Victor turned to Sami. 'Sami, whatever is the matter?' He leaned in on his cane.

She sniffed and stepped away from him, saying, 'I lost something . . . but it's all right now.'

They stood in silence as Victor raised himself up again. 'Well, I've lost something too. Have you seen that stupid bird, Pigalle? I thought I saw a crow fly out of the tunnel.'

Naz squeezed Sami's hand tightly and shook her head.

'We saw a bat, but no crows, Monsieur Rottier,' said Edie, fibbing. 'And are you sure the crow you think you saw was Pigalle anyway? They all look *so* alike.'

'Maybe that is so. Blasted bird! He'll be drumsticks before he knows it!' Victor laughed. A nasty laugh, Edie thought.

'He got into my studio last night and disturbed my precious work,' Victor went on. 'But, as you say Sami, "it's all right now". I've got something to replace what was . . . broken.'

Edie and Fabien looked at each other. Victor clearly thought it was Pigalle who had somehow accidentally allowed Leon and Souris to escape, but they were beginning to feel very uncomfortable about whatever it was he had found to replace them.

'You said you had seen my grandmother?' asked Fabien.

'Ah, yes. I asked your delightful grandmother, Madame Cloutier, if I might have a special tour around *le service des objets trouvés* earlier this afternoon, as you've all been so helpful. And it was most interesting!' he said. 'She showed me all sorts of nooks and crannies.'

Edie felt a horrible icy chill clawing its way into her bones and Fabien looked as if he might explode.

'What an intriguing place it is,' Victor went on. 'And I found *exactly* what I was looking for.' He fingered the neck of his shirt and Edie caught sight of the eyeglass chain around his neck. Even worse, she had a horrible feeling that he had a collecting box hidden in the folds of his coat.

'Well, I must be getting on. Can't waste time on a stupid bird.'

He turned and started to walk quite fast back the way he'd come.

'Fabien! I think he's got his collecting box with him,' Edie said.

Fabien pushed Napoleon into Sami's arms and took a few steps after Victor with Edie close behind him, but a line of joggers entered the tunnel and they had to press into the side to let them pass. By the time the two children were free of them, Victor was halfway up the steps to the road above.

'Monsieur Rottier, wait!' Fabien shouted.

His words were lost and as Fabien and Edie reached the top of the steps they could only watch as Victor pulled away from the kerb in a taxi and was swallowed up by the traffic.

They rushed back down to the tunnel to join the others.

'Edie, we have to get back to the Lost Property Office to find out what Victor's done,' Fabien said, clipping on Napoleon's lead. 'My grandmother will be waiting for us. Naz and Sami – you should go back to the Hotel Esmeralda. Let's hope the crazy crow has gone there.'

Naz nodded, but Sami had started crying again, quietly this time, with the tears trickling off the end of her nose. 'This is all my fault.'

Edie bent down and took her hand. 'It's all right, Sami. We'll get Pea and Impy back, because, whatever you all think of Pigalle, I don't believe he's still working for Victor.'

Chapter
Twenty-eight

Rue des Morillons

Madame Cloutier greeted Fabien and Edie at the main door, and it wasn't long before their worst fears were confirmed.

'Well, here are our musketeers!' she said. 'And how was Jardin des Plantes?'

Fabien's voice sounded as taut as a guitar string. 'It was OK, *Mamie*,' he said. 'And how was your afternoon?'

'*Très bien, merci.* And guess what? Mister Winter and I had a special visitor – the Glass House Man himself! He asked for a special guided tour of the Lost Property Office and made a very generous donation.'

Edie felt sick to the stomach.

'Where did you take him?' said Fabien.

'Oh, he wanted to see everywhere, and he asked *lots* of questions.'

Edie and Fabien looked at each other with increasing alarm.

Madame Cloutier went on. 'He got lost at one point. He wanted to use the bathroom and it was twenty minutes before he found his way back to us again. He was most *charmant* . . . if a little odd!'

'Yes!' said Dad. 'Certainly a little odd. Well, now you're here, Edie, we should be getting back to the hotel. I feel quite exhausted, but thank you once again, Madame Cloutier. What a day we've had!'

'I've just left something in Fabien's office,' Edie said. 'I won't be long.'

She and Fabien sprinted out of the reception area and round to the back door, pulling Napoleon behind them. They ran up to Fabien's cubby-hole office to find the door wide open and Enzo and Mousette's kitchen empty. Two pots were upturned on the floor and Mousette's bicycle was lying on one side.

'Please, no!' said Fabien.

Edie desperately scanned the room for Nid. At this rate they would be returning to London with no flits at all. How would Flum and the others ever forgive her?

Fabien tapped away at the pipes for what seemed like hours.

'Enzo? Mousette?' he called inside, but there was no sign of them.

Napoleon, who had been sniffing around the floor, suddenly put his paws up against the wall. Fabien lifted him up to the pipework and he pressed his nose against it and barked.

'Something's in there!' said Fabien.

They heard a tiny clatter and then Nid stuck his head out of the mouth of the pipe. His clothes were torn and there was a scrap of netting stuck in his hair. He was holding a piece of marzipan mouse.

'Nid, what happened?' Edie said. 'Where are Enzo and Mousette?'

Nid told them through dramatic hand gestures that both Enzo and Mousette had been captured by a man with a huge eye. The marzipan mouse was clearly involved and a struggle with a net, but Nid had managed to escape and hide in the pipes. Fabien looked like he might cry.

'Was the man like Vera Creech?' said Edie, and Nid nodded, circling his own eye with his fingers. Edie cupped her hand and Nid jumped onto it and folded himself up into a small ball. He looked scared and tired. She didn't dare tell him about Pigalle and Impy and Pea.

She turned to Fabien and tried to be practical.

'I'm going to have to go now with Dad. What time shall we meet?'

'I'm staying with Mamie and she usually goes to bed early. I'll go and collect Albert first and then I'll meet you in front of your hotel at nine p.m.'

Edie tried not to think too hard about how she was going to once again sneak out unnoticed by Dad. She would work that out later. 'What about the vinegar and the baking soda and all the things that Albert needs?'

'There's some here in the kitchen,' Fabien said. 'I'll bring them with me.' He looked at Edie, but no longer as if he knew all the answers. 'We *have* to get them all back, before the Big Reveal tomorrow.'

'Yes,' said Edie. 'We do.'

Chapter Twenty-nine

Hotel Esmeralda

Sami was hovering by the door of the hotel with Naz when Edie got back.

'Pigalle's not here,' she said in a stricken voice.

'I keep telling her that maybe they couldn't find the hotel,' said Naz. 'That park was quite a long way from here.'

'But then where are they?' wobbled Sami.

Luckily Nid was fast asleep in Edie's pocket and hadn't heard a word of this.

'I'm sure we'll find them soon,' said Edie calmly, but inside she felt her stomach clench up like a fist. Maybe she had got it wrong and Pigalle was just a puppet for Victor and the whole incident in the tunnel on the Promenade Plantée was part of their plan. If that was the case then Pigalle would most likely have taken Impy and Pea to Victor's shop. She couldn't bear to think about the rest.

She was relieved when Dad suggested an early supper of chicken and frites at a nearby brasserie and by eight p.m. they were walking back to the hotel. Sami, who usually ate slowly as she talked so much, had finished her meal first in virtual silence.

'Is Sami all right?' Dad asked.

'She's fine. Just tired,' said Naz, faking a huge yawn.

'We're going to have an early night, Dad,' said Edie.

'Good idea, Edie,' said Dad. 'An early night it is. We'll have breakfast together and then we have to leave for the Eurostar train mid-morning.'

They said goodnight to Dad on the stairs and then ran on up to their room to get some warm clothes. Sami's tears started again.

'We'll find them,' said Edie, doing her best to sound calm. She didn't want Sami to know how worried she was too, so she sat on the bed and fiddled with her shoelaces. There was a whoosh of water from the bathroom tap as Naz helped Sami wash her hands. Over the top of it, Edie heard a faint tapping sound.

'What's that?' said Edie.

Naz turned off the tap and they all stopped talking and listened. The sound was a little more urgent this time and it was coming from the window. Edie pulled back the curtain and immediately saw Impy's face pressed up against the glass with Pea on her back. She unlatched the window and pulled it open to let them in.

'PEA!' shouted Sami, rushing over.

Pea was looking bright-eyed as she clambered down from Impy's back and ran up Sami's arm to sit in the crook of her elbow.

'We flew so high up and saw the whole of Paris!' she said, her voice trilling like a flute. And then she added sadly, 'But Impy got hurt.'

Impy collapsed onto Edie's hand clutching her leg. Edie gently lifted Impy's hand with her finger and saw a nasty gash. She lay Impy on the bed against the pillow and, finding a cotton wool bud, she dabbed gently at the wound.

'We got lost,' Impy said. 'I was trying to guide Pigalle back here but I couldn't remember exactly where the hotel was so we flew in circles for a while. Then I remembered the bridge over the river and the big church so we followed the river until we saw Notre Dame. We were just above the giant bell towers when we were attacked by another crow.'

'It dive-bombed us,' said Pea dramatically.

'The crow was probably guarding its territory,' Naz said. 'I've seen them do that in London.'

'It caught me in the leg with its claw,' said Impy. 'But Pigalle was fast. He dropped down onto the balcony just below the bell tower and allowed us to slip off his back before the crow attacked again.'

'There were statues up there,' said Pea. 'With faces.'

'Those are gargoyles,' said Edie.

'We crept to the edge of the tower,' Impy carried on. 'We could see that Pigalle had managed to escape the first crow, but then a second crow attacked. And they fought in mid-air in a tangle of wings and claws and screeching cries, and then they dropped downwards out of sight. We couldn't see over the edge of the bell tower so we don't know what happened to Pigalle.'

Impy paused for a moment and shifted her leg. 'We stayed hidden behind the gargoyles in case the crows saw us. I could see the roof of the hotel and knew that I could fly here, but I decided to wait until it was dark.'

Edie found a handkerchief and tore off a strip of cotton. Very gently she bound Impy's leg. The relief of having Impy back made her want to weep.

'We thought Pigalle might have taken you to Victor's shop.'

'No! Pigalle was brave,' said Pea. 'He wanted to keep us safe.'

In the distance a church bell chimed the quarter hour: 8.45 p.m.

'We have to go,' said Edie.

Impy tried to stand on her newly bound leg and then crumpled again. Nid, who had woken up and crawled out of Edie's pocket, knelt down beside her, patting her shoulder.

'Not you, Impy. You have to rest,' Edie said.

For once Impy said nothing and leant back against the pillow.

'I'll stay with them,' said Naz. 'I've got some antiseptic cream that Mum gave me. I'll look after Impy and take care of that cut. Nid can help me.'

'Pea and I are coming though,' said Sami. She was already tugging on her coat and fishing the matchbox out of her pocket.

'Pea is *not* coming and neither are you!' said Edie. 'Sami, you have to be sensible! It's really dangerous! I thought you understood that now.'

For a moment it looked as if Sami might stamp her foot, but she didn't. She set the matchbox down beside Impy on the bed.

'I do understand,' she said. 'I'll leave Pea behind. But please let *me* come. I want to help. I'll do everything you say, Edie. I promise. I could be a lookout.'

Edie looked at Sami and for the first time there was an understanding between them. Sami had changed and so had she. She was changing all the time. She understood now how tangled and complicated her feelings about Fabien, Naz, Sami and the flits had been, and she didn't want to be like the crow that attacked Pigalle – angry and territorial.

'What about Mum?' said Naz. 'I promised her . . .'

'It's OK,' said Edie. 'I'll look after Sami. I'll make a promise too.'

Together they put on their coats and hats.

A pebble hit the window with a sharp *ting*.

'Fabien's here. We need to go.'

Chapter Thirty

Passage de Curiosité

The three of them walked quickly over the bridge. It was another cold, clear night and a half-moon cast a pale silvery-blue light over the two bell towers of Notre Dame.

'Wait,' said Edie, pausing. 'I just need a few minutes.'

She told Fabien what had happened with Pigalle and ran across the flagstones in front of the great cathedral, craning her neck to look up at the towers. She could just see the ancient gargoyles rearing out from the sides of the building and the winged shoulders of the chimera grotesques with their fixed stony faces. The balcony under the bell towers was incredibly high. If Pigalle was brave, then Impy and Pea were too. She lowered her eyes, searching out the nooks and crannies and shadowy corners at the base of the cathedral, half expecting to see the crow's crumpled body.

'Pigalle!' she called. 'Pigalle!' She rattled the last of the seed in the paper bag in her pocket, but there was no sign of him.

*

When they reached Passage de Curiosité, the passage-way was deserted and the shops closed up, with the only light coming from the toyshop window as before. They walked carefully along to Victor's shop in case he was there, but the blind was drawn and there were no lights on upstairs. Fabien carefully put down the bag he had been carrying and opened the zip a little.

'Albert? Are you OK?'

'I'm fine! Just a little seasick,' a voice answered back. 'Are we there yet?'

'We're just waiting for the others.'

Fabien opened the zip a little more and Edie could see Albert sitting inside a cardboard box, surrounded by strange packages and dropper bottles. A tub of baking soda, vinegar and a couple of torches were tucked in beside the box.

'Leon and Souris should be here soon,' said Fabien.

They looked up and down the deserted passage-way. They could hear footsteps crossing the boulevard at the far end and the distant sound of traffic. They waited for a few minutes, but Edie was impatient to go around to the back of the shop to Pigalle's tree and see if he was there.

'Why don't we go and check –' she started.

'Wait!' said Sami. She had crouched down and was looking along the line of the shops where the doors met the tiled walkway.

They all looked and saw a clutch of tiny flames dotted around a vent in the wall. It was next to the bookshop at the top. They took a few steps towards it and saw twenty or maybe thirty flits tumbling down a makeshift ramp, pushing their bicycles before them and each holding a lit match. As their matches sputtered and burnt out they piled them up on the side of the walkway. Then the peloton of cyclists reformed into a neat group and came pedalling towards them. Each flit wore a coloured shirt and a cap and Leon was at the front wearing a shirt of yellow and green. The cyclists circled around Fabien's, Edie's and Sami's feet.

'It's like the Tour de France!' said Sami, her eyes widening.

'*Je suis désolé!*' Leon said. 'We are late, I know, but it was very dark under the museum and there were so many drains and tunnels.' He turned and whistled and out of the vent came two Metro mice, grimy like the London Underground mice, but not quite as bold. They clung to the sides of the passageway and were wary of the human children, briefly pausing to rifle through an abandoned sandwich bag.

'Marais mice,' Leon said proudly. 'They knew the way and they protected us from the rats.'

The cyclists came to a standstill.

'Where is Albert the Apothecary?' Leon asked.

'In here!' called Albert, and Fabien patted the bag.

'*Alors!* We have no time to lose if we are to rescue Violette,' Leon said, turning towards Victor Rottier's shop. The door did not quite reach the bottom, leaving a gap of about two or three centimetres.

'We can go under here,' said Leon. 'But how will you get in?'

'There's a way in around the back,' said Fabien, zipping up his bag again.

Edie held up the key to the back door that she had taken from its ring only the night before. 'We'll see you inside.'

One by one the cyclists disappeared under the door and, when they were all safely inside, Fabien, Sami and Edie ran to the end of the tiled walkway. As a nearby church struck ten o'clock, they had pushed open

the gate at the back of Passage de Curiosité and were running towards Pigalle's tree. The spindly branches were empty.

'I think the other crow may have killed him,' said Edie, imagining his broken body lying on the side of a street or in the valley of a Parisian rooftop.

'I got him wrong too,' said Fabien. 'It sounds like he was very brave.'

Kraaa! The cry was cracked and weak, but it was unmistakable.

'Pigalle?'

Edie ran towards the back wall and there between the bins was a cage, and inside was Pigalle, tangled up in some netting.

Kraaa! he said sadly when he saw them.

Edie put her finger through the bars of the cage and tried to stroke the feathers on his head. The bird tried to move forward but his wings were tightly bound by the net. One of his eyes was half closed and she could see dried blood all over his neck and a bald patch where the other crow must have pulled out his feathers.

'What happened to you?' she said.

The cage was locked from the outside, so she unbolted the door and wrapped her hand around Pigalle's body, gently lifting him out. The netting around his wings was bound by an elastic band.

'Victor must have done this! He must want to stuff him like the others. That's what he's been planning all along.'

'We won't let him,' said Sami.

Kraaa! squawked Pigalle weakly.

Edie took the last of the seeds out of her pocket.

'You need food, Pigalle,' she said. She held a seed up to his beak and Pigalle took it.

'Look!' said Fabien. He pointed up to the window, where the light of a match told him that the other flits were waiting. 'We have to go inside.'

They unlocked the door and Sami and Fabien turned on the torches and hurried upstairs.

Edie carried Pigalle inside and laid him on the counter by the sink. She turned on the light. Its dusty yellow bulb cast a dim, sickly glow that couldn't be seen from the shop front, but it was enough for her to work with. She pulled open the drawers until she found a pair of kitchen scissors and then she gently cut through the elastic band and the netting to free Pigalle. He fluffed and flapped his wings. He was missing a few tail feathers, and the wounds around his neck and head were nasty and deep. She found a first-aid kit under the sink and, after pouring antiseptic onto some cotton wool, she dabbed at the wounds to clean them. Perhaps, she thought as she worked, Albert could make a poultice for Pigalle. Then she gave Pigalle a long drink of water and a piece of dried baguette from the bread bin.

Kraaa! he said once again, shaking out his feathers. His cry was stronger now and his eyes had recovered some of their brightness.

'Edie!' Fabien called in a harsh whisper from the bottom of the steps. 'We need you!'

Edie opened the back door and put Pigalle on the ground.

'Fly away, Pigalle. Fly a long, long way from Victor and don't come back.' She watched as he hopped out into the yard and lurched upwards into the branches of the tree.

Chapter
Thirty-one

Passage de Curiosité

When Edie got upstairs, the door of the cold store was open with its blue light spilling out into the storeroom.

'I can't find them,' Fabien said. He had clearly been hoping that Enzo and Mousette might still be trapped in Victor's collecting box, but the workbench was empty. They lifted the first of the three glass dioramas onto the workbench and turned on a small lamp. All the flits, including Albert, stared in horror as the carousel lit up in all its sickly glitter and the Christmas reindeer slowly turned to a soundtrack of tinny music with frozen enamelled flits on their backs.

'It's much worse than we ever imagined,' one of the Bastille cyclists said.

Fabien and Edie went back into the cold store to fetch the circus scene. There was a cloth draped over the top of it, so they set it alongside the winter scene and pulled off the cloth. The circus set appeared to have had a fresh coat of red and gold paint and the acrobats, the clown and the trapeze artist were still there with Violette juggling, but there were also some new figures dressed in circus outfits. Fabien gave a strangled cry and gripped his hand into a fist. Dreadful as it was, it was exactly as they had anticipated. Victor's trip to the Lost Property Office was far from the innocent visit he had proposed to Madame Cloutier. There, alongside Violette, were two new jugglers – Enzo and Mousette! There was a stunned silence as Edie, Fabien, Sami and all the flits took in this second scene, horror etched on their faces.

'It's horrible!' said Sami. 'I hate him. I don't know why I ever liked him.'

'He puts on a good act,' said Edie. 'But now we know what he's really like, we have to get the flits out of their prison.' She tried again to lift the glass domes from their plinth, but both were locked. She looked at the size of the keyholes.

'Sami, we have to find the keys that open them. They must be very small.' She took one of the torches and together they went back into the main studio. The ring of keys that Edie had taken the back-door key from wasn't there any more, so they started to pull open the drawers under the workbench. There were all the tools that Victor used for his work – the tweezers, the spikes, the needle and thread, the scissors and brushes. Even the eyeglass was hanging from its hook, but there were no small keys.

'Wait,' said Sami. 'I'm sure I saw some when we were last here.' She closed her eyes for a moment and then leapt forward, running to the end of the desk where Victor kept the packets of bird seed for Pigalle. She plunged her hand into the seed box, pushing aside a paper bag of nuts, and pulled out a red ribbon. There, dangling on the end, were three silver keys.

'Sami! That's brilliant,' said Edie as Sami handed her the ribbon.

'And now I'm going to stay here by the window,' said Sami. 'In case he comes. I said I'd be your lookout.'

Edie nodded and rushed back through the curtain to find that Fabien had brought the third glass dome out of the cold store. Edie tried each key until all three glass covers were unlocked. They lifted the circus dome off first.

Leon climbed up onto the set and tried to wrap his arms around Violette, but her arms and legs were like those of a china doll. Fabien touched Mousette with the tip of his finger, but the normally energetic flit didn't move a muscle, and Albert stood in front of Enzo, staring at him. The cold store had set the enamel varnish and it was now completely solid.

'*Mon pauvre frère,*' was all he said. 'My poor dear brother.'

The tools of Victor's trade – the cans of Polar Freeze spray that he used to fix them into position, the pot of transparent enamel varnish and the tube of extra-strong glue – lay on his workbench. Fabien swept them all into a bag.

'Let's try to unglue them first,' Edie said. She helped Albert onto the bench and began to set up his apothecary under the lamp. He spread out his potions and tiny dropper bottles.

'We must mix together the vinegar and baking soda on a saucer,' he said. Edie found a saucer in the kitchen and stirred the two together to form a paste. Albert added several drops of lemon juice from a pipette.

Then Edie took one of Victor's camel-haired brushes and began covering each blob of glue around the flits' feet with the paste and waited.

Albert now began to make up a potion that would loosen the enamel varnish and Fabien found a coffee cup on a shelf in Victor's studio that would work as the 'dipping' bath. Fabien put in a tablespoon of vinegar and then Albert added safflower oil, rosemary, orange peel and lavender oil, and other powdered dried leaves and plant essences, though Edie had no idea what they were. He added a mixture of water, sugar and brewer's yeast that he always had ready in Jardin des Plantes using a distilling jar, a funnel and some copper tubing. The mixture looked all gooey as he poured it into the dipping bath.

'This should do it,' said Albert.

Edie's paste was starting to work and the glue was slowly dissolving. As each flit was unstuck from their theatrical sets, Leon and Souris and the peloton of cyclists from Bastille tipped each figure up and carried them to the bath where they lined them up in a row to be treated by Albert and Fabien.

The trapeze artist was first in line. Fabien lifted him into the coffee cup and gently swilled the mixture around him right up to his neck, while Albert took a small brush and painted the gooey liquid all over his face and hair.

They all watched, but nothing happened.

'It might take a little time,' said Albert. He took off his glasses and rubbed them, then dabbed at his forehead with his handkerchief. Then he hummed a tune as everyone waited.

Edie bit her lip. What if it didn't work?

Albert noticed it first. A tiny wiggle in the tips of the trapeze artist's fingers. Shortly afterwards the enamel on his arms began to soften and crack and the flit lifted one arm up and waved it about excitedly.

As it dissolved from his legs, he jiggled his knees up and down, and as the horrible varnish melted away from his face and hair he stood up, coughing and spluttering but beaming from ear to ear.

'Thank you,' he said, clinging onto Albert. 'Thank you.'

Violette was next in line and Leon and Souris stood beside her, waiting.

'At least she feels warmer,' said Leon.

'I saw her eyes move!' said Souris, and Violette gave another tiny blink of her eyes; in the corner of each a tear had formed. After a few minutes in the bath she too was free of her casing. The Bastille cyclists cheered, and Leon and Souris threw their arms around their sister.

It was like an assembly line in a factory – the figures were carefully unglued and lined up for the dipping bath. One by one the flits emerged out of their enamelled shells.

'We knew we were alive,' said Mousette. 'But we couldn't move at all. We could have been stuck in that awful scene forever.'

Albert stood among them in his green lab coat with his arm around Enzo's shoulder. 'I think the varnish made your clothes, hair and skin visible to adults, but they would only ever see your shiny covering. You were lucky that Victor didn't paint over your eyes – by blinking you raised the alarm.'

'There's one more thing I have to do,' Fabien announced. He pulled out a large packet of sweets from the bottom of his bag. They were jelly babies – moulded jelly figures of green and red and yellow. Picking up the tube of Victor's glue, he then stuck a jelly baby wherever there had been an enamelled flit. In time they would dissolve into nothing more than sugary goo.

The flits laughed and cheered as Edie and Fabien lifted back the heavy glass dome lids and locked them in place, carrying them over to Victor's desk in the main studio, ready to greet him in the morning. The day of the Big Reveal.

'And *I've* got one more thing to do too,' said Edie. She snatched the eyeglass from its hook by Victor's workbench and, pulling open a drawer, she took out a hammer.

'If I smash it, he won't even be able to *see* any flits at all, let alone make them a part of his horrible miniature scenes.'

Once again the flits cheered her on and stamped the ground.

'Edie!' Sami suddenly shouted from her perch on the window seat. 'It's Victor! He's coming down the passage.'

She jumped away from the window and crouched down.

There was complete silence as they all looked at each other, as still and rigid as Victor's enamelled figures.

'The light!' whispered Edie.

Fabien sprinted back into the storeroom to switch off the lamp and shut the door of the cold store. In the sudden gloom Sami took two steps towards Victor's worktable.

'Quick, Leon and Souris. I need your help.' Without questioning it they jumped onto her hand.

'Sami, what are you doing?' whispered Edie anxiously. But Sami turned and ran across the studio and down the stairs just as the key turned in the lock.

There was a gasp of surprise as the light was switched on and Victor was greeted by Sami.

'Agh! Sami, what are you doing here?' His surprise quickly turned to anger. 'How did you get in?'

Sami's voice rose up the stairs, full of the innocence she had felt on the first day she had met him.

'Hello, Mr Victor. I was waiting for you because I've found some more flits! Look!'

'What's she doing?' mouthed Fabien.

Edie shrugged, but she was worried. She hoped that Sami wasn't going to try to bargain with a man like Victor Rottier.

'Well, that is kind, Sami. Thank you.' He no longer

seemed bothered as to how Sami had got inside his shop. 'And yes, I'd like them very much. Please put them here in my hand.'

Then there was a clatter as the door was pulled open again and the scramble of feet.

'You'll have to catch me first!' shouted Sami, and she ran out into the street.

They could hear Victor muttering, 'Stupid English girl!' but the bait worked as he ran out after her and the shop door shut with a bang. They could hear her light footsteps running up the tiled passageway and his heavy ones as he ran after her.

'Genius!' said Fabien. 'She's giving us time to get everyone out of here!'

It *was* genius, Edie agreed, but the thought of what would happen if Victor managed to catch up with Sami filled her with terror.

Chapter
Thirty-two

Passage de Curiosité

Everyone assembled on the studio table. There was now a group of almost fifty flits and only ten bicycles propped up downstairs where the Bastille cyclists had left them.

'How do we get everyone out of here?' said Fabien. 'I could carry everyone in my bag.'

'We can't leave until I know that Sami is safe,' said Edie firmly. 'But the flits must get away at once. Can each cyclist take a passenger? And there's Leon's and Souris's bikes too.'

'And the mice?' said Fabien. 'Maybe they could carry two as well?'

They hurried downstairs and found the mice outside in the passageway near the vent, hoovering up the crumbs from a forgotten brioche.

'Quick!' said Fabien. 'You have to leave NOW.' The Bastille cyclists slipped under the door, each with a flit passenger, and in a long line pedalled down to the vent and up the ramp. The mice followed behind with four more flits riding on their backs and clinging to the tips of their ears. Edie and Fabien watched until they were all safely through the vent, leaving only the crumbs of brioche behind.

There were still another ten flits left.

'We haven't got much time left,' said Fabien. 'Perhaps they should just run for it?'

There was a tap on the window upstairs. Edie dashed back up thinking it might be Sami, but instead she saw Pigalle's face at the glass. Quickly she pulled one side of the window open.

'Pigalle, you *must* go like I told you! Victor's here now!' But Pigalle didn't move. Edie noticed that just beyond him, sitting in the branches of the tree, were three other crows. One of them hopped onto the sill beside Pigalle and gently groomed his feathers.

'Are these friends?' Edie asked.

Pigalle flew up onto her shoulder as he had done in the tunnel and the crows flew in after him and stood in an expectant row on Victor's desk. Pigalle stretched out his wings and Edie suddenly realised what he was trying to do.

'Fabien!' she yelled. 'Pigalle is going to help us!'

Fabien's head appeared at the bottom of the stairs and he looked warily at the dusty line of birds.

'Can we really trust them?' he said.

'Yes!' said Edie. 'Yes, we can. And besides, do you have a better plan?'

'No,' Fabien said, grinning.

He hurried up the stairs with the remaining flits and, one by one, they lifted them onto the crows' backs, instructing them to cling to the feathers and to each other. Finally, Fabien lifted Enzo, Albert the Apothecary and Mousette onto the third crow's back. Only Violette was left.

'I have to wait for my brothers,' she said. 'I can't return to Bastille without them.'

'Pigalle should wait too,' said Edie. 'Just in case you and your brothers need to make a quick escape.'

'Take the *volettes* to the Lost Property Office,' Fabien said to the other three crows. 'Rue des Morillons.' One by one, the crows perched on the windowsill and lifted off, stretching their wings out and flying upwards into the Parisian sky.

'Now we need to hide,' Fabien said.

Edie spotted the hammer she had dropped when Sami raised the alarm.

'The eyeglass!' she said.

Once again she picked up the hammer, but there was a frantic banging on the back door. Edie ran down with Violette and found Sami very short of breath and holding the stitch in her side. She helped her through into the main shop.

'I think I've lost him,' she said. 'But we have to get out of here before he comes back.'

'Do you still have Leon and Souris?' asked Violette.

'Yes!' said Sami, opening her fist to show Violette the two flits in her hand.

'Quick, back upstairs!' said Fabien.

There was a jangle of keys and the front door was flung open. The shop bell almost flew off its hinges and lights snapped on all over the shop.

'Sami!' yelled Victor Rottier. Heavy steps came thumping up the stairs and there he was in his long coat and crocodile boots. One of his trouser legs was torn and he was limping, but in his raised arm he held his cane.

'Give me those *volettes*!' he said and waved his cane above his head. Sami stepped forward and stood in front of him.

'Never!' shouted Sami. 'You are a horrible man.'

'Well, young Sami!' Victor said with a nasty undertone. 'You seem to have changed your mind about me.'

Then he caught sight of Edie and Fabien on the far side of the studio table.

'You're here too!' he said, then his eyes roved beyond them and his face hardened as he saw the open curtain to the storeroom. Fabien hadn't closed the door of the cold store properly and it slowly swung open, spilling out its strange blue light.

Then Victor spotted the three glass dome shapes on his worktable.

'What have you done?' he asked quietly. His voice was icy cold.

'We've made some changes!' said Fabien calmly, but Edie could see that his hand was shaking as he lifted the cloth off each of the three domes.

Victor stared at the broken and damaged sets and the lurid jelly babies stuck where his precious enamelled flits had been. There was a deathly silence as he took in the full transformation of his Big Reveal.

'You have made a mockery of my work,' he thundered. 'Where are my *volettes*?'

'They're not *your volettes*. They don't belong to you!' shouted Fabien. 'We've freed them all!'

'Freed them?' Victor took a moment to recover himself and narrowed his eyes. 'Well then, I shall find some more.

You cannot stop me.' He added in a wheedling voice, 'They are my friends. They *like* what I do.'

He glanced up at the pegs on the wall.

'Are you looking for this?' Edie said, holding up the eyeglass.

'I'd give that back if I were you,' said Victor, cold and steely again. He leaned towards her with an outstretched hand and Edie could see the spittle on his lips.

'We know exactly what you did,' she said, moving back. 'You were stealing flits, just like Vera Creech.'

'So you know Vera!' said Victor.

'She worked for my dad at the Lost Property Office in London,' said Edie. 'It was me and my friend Charlie who caught her.'

'So you're the meddling girl in the newspaper articles. I might have guessed!'

'How do *you* know Vera?' Fabien asked.

'Vera Creech is my English cousin and she was my inspiration for . . . all this!' Victor gestured towards the glass domes. 'Such a clever idea to use the flits as pickpockets. Wish I'd thought of it myself. But as Edie knows only too well, Vera was also careless. It was my grandfather who originally gave her the eyeglass,' he went on. 'The story goes that he bought it from a man who ran a flea circus on the Left Bank. Vera showed me that you could see the little creatures through it, and it was Pigalle who rescued it when Vera was caught and brought it to me!'

Edie sensed Pigalle shifting under the table.

'And, just like Vera, you chose to make money out of the flits rather than help them,' she said.

'I have a business to run!'

'At the expense of others. I heard you lying to that rich boy's father. You were pretending that you had "made" the flits, as if you're some brilliant artist. Instead, you were stealing them by catching them in your net.'

'But I am an artist!'

'You're not! You're a thief just like your stupid cousin, and I'm going to make sure you never see them again,' said Edie, and she placed the eyeglass on the table. Victor lunged forward, but Edie had already pulled the hammer from her pocket and smashed the eyeglass into a thousand tiny pieces. She swept the shards of glass into her hat.

'Noo!' said Victor and he put his hands up to his face in a theatrical fashion. Then he began to laugh horribly, like a villain in a pantomime.

'You silly girl! Did you think that was the only one?'

He opened his coat to reveal another eyeglass chain around his neck.

'I forgot to mention that my grandfather had two eyeglasses. He left one to Vera and one to me. I shall go out and catch more flits to replace those you useless children have freed, but why don't I make a start with the ones that Sami has brought for me.'

He lunged towards Sami.

'Look out!' shouted Edie.

'Run!' Violette shouted from her hiding place in the seed box, but it was too late. Victor had grasped Sami's wrist in a vice-like grip only inches from where Leon and Souris were hiding. Holding the second eyeglass up to his eye he forced open her hand and caught Souris between his finger and thumb.

'Not Souris!' cried Leon.

A whir of black feathers flew up from under the table, clawing and pecking at Victor's face. He let go of Sami and stumbled backwards.

'Pigalle! How did you escape? You hateful bird.' Victor waved his cane around, but Pigalle ducked under his arm and attacked again, beating his wings and jabbing with his beak, forcing Victor back down the stairs. Pigalle was trying to pluck the second eyeglass from around his neck.

'What are you doing, Pigalle? You should be fighting *them*!' Victor cried out.

Victor pressed the silver top on his cane and out sprang the net, which caught in Pigalle's outstretched claws and the bird became entangled. Victor dropped the cane but with the eyeglass still in place around his neck

and Souris caught between his thumb and forefinger he pulled open the door and ran out of the shop.

'He's got Souris,' cried Sami from the top of the stairs.

'Quick!' said Fabien. 'After him.'

They ran out into the passageway and saw Victor at the far end, no longer limping and moving surprisingly fast.

'We can't let him get away with that eyeglass!' said Edie.

They ran on into the main street, but Victor had disappeared.

Chapter Thirty-three

Passage de Curiosité to the **River Seine**

Back in the shop, Sami was on her knees trying to disentangle Pigalle. Some of his tail feathers were caught fast in the net and he was struggling to escape.

'Keep still, Pigalle!'

'Please hurry,' said Violette. 'So he can go after Souris.'

'Careful, Sami!' said Fabien. 'He won't be able to fly properly if you damage his feathers.'

Leon and Violette clambered in among the netting, using their tiny fingers to help free him, and at last Pigalle wriggled out with the wounds around his neck bleeding again. His tail feathers, although slightly askew, were still intact. He hopped into the passageway and, after an unsteady lurch to the side, he took off after Victor.

Sami swept the two remaining Bastille flits into her

pocket and, with Edie and Fabien, they all followed him, running across the empty street and craning their necks upwards to see where Pigalle was. The sodium glow of the streetlamps made it difficult to see, but the night was still clear and moonlit.

'There he is,' said Edie.

The bird was circling above them, looking for Victor and making wider and wider loops like a drone camera to cover the surrounding streets. They all watched him until quite suddenly he made a sharp left turn and dropped downwards.

'I think he's found Victor,' said Fabien and he sprinted off ahead of the others.

Edie and Sami ran after him, turning right off the main boulevard. They saw Pigalle again silhouetted against the inky blue of the night sky. He was zig-zagging back and forth and wheeling around, but he was definitely following something as he led them into a maze of smaller streets that wound their way towards the river. They ran past empty shops and cafés, twisting this way and that until Edie had to stop, gasping for air and clutching her side.

'I'll catch you up,' she called to Sami and Fabien. She tried to catch her breath as she heard their footsteps fading into the distance. A dustcart slowly lumbered up the street and she pressed herself to one side to let it pass. She knew the French dustmen might think it odd to see a twelve-year-old girl out alone at night so she made sure she remained hidden. They worked their way along the café bins and she looked down at the hat she was still holding in her hand, filled with the broken shards of the eyeglass.

When the dustmen weren't looking, she quickly tipped it into the mechanical mouth at the back of the lorry and listened to the scrunching sound as the glass was digested along with all the other rubbish.

Edie took a couple of deep breaths and started to jog again, turning left and then right until up ahead she saw Sami half running and half walking down a narrow cobbled street. Fabien was nowhere to be seen. At the end of the street Edie could see the sky opening up over the river and the artists' stalls that lined the river wall.

'Sami, wait for me!' she called out and Sami turned, but as she did there was a violent clatter of bins and Victor leapt out of a shadowy doorway and caught hold of her coat.

'Give me those other *volettes*!' he shouted, tugging hard. Sami stumbled and fell.

'Leave her alone!' cried Edie, pushing her legs to run faster, but before she could reach Sami, Pigalle swooped over her head like a storm cloud in a driving wind.

This time he lifted up into the air and divebombed Victor from above, pulling at his hair and pecking at his neck. Victor lurched forward and sprawled onto the cobbles just beyond Sami and as he fell Souris tumbled out of his hand. Pigalle dived down once again and plucked the eyeglass from Victor's neck.

'Give that back!' shouted Victor, and this time there was real panic in his voice, but Pigalle flew upwards and perched on a second-floor window. The eyeglass chain hung from his beak.

'You hateful do-good children,' said Victor fumbling around on the cobbles for Souris. 'Where is that *volette*?'

But without the eyeglass Victor couldn't see Souris and Sami had already crawled forward and swept him up into the folds of her coat. Edie helped her back up again.

'Are all the Bastille flits safe now?' she whispered and Sami nodded.

Victor turned his attention back to the crow and pulled a paper bag of nuts from his coat pocket.

'You can have all these, Pigalle. And there's more back at my shop. Lots more. Just give me the eyeglass back.' He spoke with a wheedling charm.

Pigalle cocked his head to one side, then shook out his wings and lifted off again towards the river.

'Come back, you disobedient bird!' yelled Victor, taking off after him, his coat flapping behind him.

'Edie, wait!' Fabien appeared at the top of the street. He had taken a wrong turning. She beckoned him quickly to follow and they crossed the *quai* that ran alongside the river and turned onto the bridge where Pigalle was now perched on the railings, dangling the eyeglass over the water.

'You wouldn't!' said Victor in a low, menacing voice, reaching out his hand.

'Go on, Pigalle! Do it,' Edie whispered.

Pigalle took off into the wide-open, moonlit sky over the river. He flew higher and higher until he was just a silhouette, and then he circled back towards them, swooping downwards over the spot where the river was at its deepest.

Then he dropped the second eyeglass.

Victor stood at the railings and stared down at the cold waters of the Seine racing underneath. This time his cry of 'Nooooo!' was real. The second eyeglass had sunk without trace.

Victor shook his fist furiously at the bird and then at the children and staggered past them, back towards the tangle of streets on the Right Bank.

Sami tugged at Edie's coat and pointed.

Pigalle was doing a victory fly-past with a loop-the-

loop, and Edie, Fabien, Sami and the French flits waved
and cheered until he finally flew off with a defiant *kraaa!*

'Look, Sami!' said Edie. 'Isn't Paris beautiful?' And
together they looked at the long line of illuminated,
twinkling bridges along the river, and in the distance the
iron finger of the Eiffel Tower lit up in gold.

Chapter Thirty-four

Paris Gare du Nord to **London St Pancras**

Quite a party was assembled under the station clock at the Gare du Nord. Madame Cloutier, Fabien and Napoleon (wearing a coat in the colours of the French flag) had come to wave them off and even Claude Epingler was there, although he was doing his best to ignore all children and dogs. Claude showed Dad where his waxwork figure would eventually be displayed, next to the stairs leading up to the Eurostar terminal. Here, Claude declared grandly, his wax scuplture would hold its ground in the 'busy current of Londoners and Parisians eddying back and forth'.

Dad turned pink with pleasure.

'And, Mr Winter,' Claude added, 'would allow us all to understand the true meaning of being lost and found!'

Fabien, Naz and Edie shared a glance, but Madame Cloutier cried, 'Bravo!' and Mr Winter seemed quite overcome. He announced that he would return during the Christmas holidays with Edie and Mum to see the waxwork when it was complete.

'You will be famous like Sherlock Holmes,' said Fabien as he shook Mr Winter by the hand. This time there was no hint of a smirk.

Fabien's bag was full as he had a number of lost-property deliveries to make, including taking Leon, Souris and Violette home to Bastille and Albert the Apothecary back to Jardin des Plantes, but it meant that the flits could also say goodbye while Claude distracted Dad and Madame Cloutier. Albert had prepared some calendula and tea tree for Impy's leg, and Enzo and Mousette presented both Impy and Nid with cycle helmets made from Parisian bottle tops and their very own bicycle. Nid was ecstatic.

There was a raucous exchange of goodbyes as their train was announced, to which Claude put his fingers in his ears with a pained expression.

Fabien turned to Edie. 'Until Christmas then?'

'Yes.'

'*Au revoir,* Edie.'

'Bye, Fabien,' said Edie. 'And I'm sorry if I seemed a bit stuck up at first. I thought you were a show-off, but you aren't. You just know a lot of things.'

'You *were* a bit stuck up,' said Fabien. 'And bossy, but you're brave too.'

Edie bent down and ruffled Napoleon's ears and Sami threw her arms around everyone except Claude.

Chapter Thirty-five

Alexandra Palace

How was Paris? I'd like to see pics. Book of Knots is great. Shall we meet usual place at Ally Pally? C

'Hi,' said Charlie, slinging his bag down on the grassy slope just below Alexandra Palace. Other Year Eights were kicking a ball about further down the hill and a knot of Year Sevens were eating crisps on a bench.

'You can see for miles up here,' said Charlie.

It was a Saturday morning and it felt warm for November. London was laid out in front of them like a fabulous rug with long threads of terraced houses stitched over with patches of green and, along the ribbon of the Thames, office blocks and cranes poked upwards like random pins.

It was Edie's favourite place.

'So what's it like being thirteen then?' she asked.

'It's no different really,' said Charlie. 'I have to do the washing up more often though.'

Edie laughed, but she could feel a tight knot forming in her stomach. What could be more different than never being able to see the flits again?

'So you don't feel like you've sort of grown up?'

'Nah!' said Charlie. He turned back from the view and looked at her. 'That's a weird thing to say. Thirteen isn't exactly grown up.'

'No. I s'pose not,' said Edie.

'Come on then. Let's see the photos.'

Edie scrolled through some of the photos on her phone, mostly the ones that Dad had taken on the morning that Madame Cloutier had shown them around Paris. Charlie chatted easily and asked lots of questions, like how many steps did it take to climb the Eiffel Tower, did they eat smelly cheese and was Sami really annoying? And he said he liked the look of Fabien as there was a photo of him standing outside the main doors of the Paris Lost Property Office. Charlie pulled a chocolate bar out of his pocket and broke off a corner for Edie.

'So what did you like best about the whole trip?'

'I liked finding out that there are French flits too!' said Edie firmly.

'Flits?' said Charlie. He said the word nervously, as if he was supposed to know what she was talking about.

'Do you know why we were there, Charlie?'

'Because your dad was getting a waxwork made,' he said. 'Because of the Lost Property Office and the ghost station at Wilde Street and all the stuff we found down there with Benedict.'

'Charlie, you must remember that it was because of the *flits* that we went to Wilde Street in the first place. You saw them too. You helped me to rescue them, and yet that time we went to the Hillside Camp with Sami and Naz just before your thirteenth birthday it was like you'd forgotten everything.'

'Edie, I look at all the photos and newspaper cuttings and I can see I was there. I remember finding all that stuff at Wilde Street and the dark, spooky ghost station and Vera Creech, but I don't remember the flits. I know when we met at Highgate Station that you were angry with me because I couldn't see something, but did they really exist?'

'YES, Charlie, they EXIST!' said Edie, buzzing like an angry wasp. 'How can you *possibly* forget them after all we went through?'

A couple of the Year Sevens nudged each other and looked across at her. Charlie went very quiet and stared hard at the view over London, and she knew she had gone too far.

'I'm sorry,' she said in a small voice. 'It's not your fault. I'm frightened, that's all. I'm thirteen next month and I'm scared the same thing is going to happen to me.'

'I just want us to be friends, Edie,' said Charlie. 'Like we were.'

'We *are* still friends, Charlie,' said Edie firmly. She knew in that moment that if being thirteen meant losing the flits then it mustn't mean losing Charlie too.

*

That night she sat at her desk and drew pictures of Impy and Nid and Enzo and Mousette, pinning them up on the cork board on her wall. And then she set out a miniature flit camp on her desk with a table made from a French soapbox packet and four French bottle tops that she'd brought back with her from Paris. Her phone pinged on her bed. It was a message from Charlie.

It might not happen to you.

She smiled and lay spreadeagled on her bed saying over and over again, 'It might not happen to me! It might not happen to me! It might not happen to me!'

And then it did.

Chapter Thirty-six

Highgate – the Hillside Camp

It began with a strange feeling.

With only three days to go before her birthday, Edie went with Naz and Sami to the Hillside Camp and, as they walked down the hill beside the Tube station, there it was – a sudden, strange feeling in the pit of her stomach that she didn't really want to go any more.

It felt like a chore, like washing up or doing maths homework, and she'd rather be doing something else. She was distracted too by her shoes that had become even tighter and more uncomfortable than they had been in Paris over half-term. Her toes pinched so much now that she started to think about new ones and what type she might try to persuade Mum and Dad to buy for her.

As they crawled through the hedge by the car park,

Edie tried to crowd out these thoughts, and concentrate only on the flits.

'Focus. Don't let go yet,' she kept saying to herself as Sami charged ahead, clutching her bag of recyling.

Edie climbed up onto the deserted platform and her vision began to blur at the edges. She pressed her fists into her eyes and rubbed them, but as she walked towards the bank, the cheery street of flit houses wavered in and out of focus.

Edie put her hand to her head.

'Are you OK?' said Naz.

'Yes, I . . . You go on ahead,' Edie said suddenly. 'I just need a minute.' She took two steps back and sat on the edge of the platform just as Charlie had done. Sami was standing on tiptoes peering into the Hillside Camp and calling out to Pea.

An ache formed in Edie's throat and hot tears slid down her cheeks. Something was happening to her, as if the tide had come in, washing around her feet, and was now drawing away, dragging her and everything with it. She didn't want to go, at least not quite yet. She felt the familiar brush of Impy's wings across her hair and there she was, hovering in front of her nose.

'Why won't you come over?' Impy demanded.

Edie said nothing and Impy leant forward and felt the damp trickle of water on Edie's face. Her bossiness gave way to bewilderment.

'Don't cry!' Impy said. 'You never cry!'

Edie turned over her hand and Impy settled herself on it, leaning against the ball of her thumb.

'This is about your thirteenth birthday, isn't it?'

'I think it's happening already,' said Edie, the words catching in her throat. 'And I thought I might be different.'

'I told you, Edie. It happens to everyone. You can't stop it. You don't want to be twelve forever,' Impy said.

'But I can't imagine you not being here,' said Edie. Impy's outline blurred and fuzzed again as if someone had smeared Vaseline across her eyes. Edie gently felt for Impy's foot with the tip of her finger and Impy pushed back.

'We'll be here. It's just you won't be able to *see* us . . . and maybe you won't want to see us either. That's just the way it goes.'

Then Impy pressed something into Edie's hand. 'It's an early birthday present,' she said.

Edie opened her palm to find a tiny flat pebble with the letters I and E scratched onto it.

Impy flew up and whispered into the shell of Edie's ear. 'I won't forget.'

Another hot tear slipped down Edie's cheek and dripped off her nose.

'Come on,' said Impy briskly.

Flying down again, she took hold of Edie's index finger and led her over to the Hillside Camp and pointed at Sami.

'That's why it's going to be OK.'

Sami's head was bent over and she was completely entranced. Her face lit up as she played with Pea, walking her fingers up and down and rolling silver beads towards her in a game of catch. Nid was trying to show her a cycle trick with the new French bicycle and Flum was sorting through the latest recycling items that Sami had brought with her – a salt cellar, some LEGO bricks, a teabag and a small tin for pins.

Naz slipped her arm through Edie's. She was a month younger than Edie so this wouldn't happen to her until the New Year. Edie smiled. Naz was one of the best things about Year Eight and she knew that their friendship would carry her through Years Nine, Ten and Eleven. That was something to look forward to, wasn't it? But for now she kept her eyes on Sami, even as the scene before her flickered on and off as if it was wired to a faulty electrical circuit.

Sami would carry on visiting the flits, making the connection that Edie might be about to lose and that Charlie had already lost. And there would be others too, like Fabien, filled with curiosity and imagination.

The light was slowly disappearing in the December afternoon and Edie wondered if they should leave, but Naz said, 'Close your eyes for a moment.'

When she opened them again, the whole camp was lit up. The terraced row of houses was dotted with a string of fairy lights and minute strips of tin foil, which glittered in the breeze. Sami had set up two large bicycle lights at either side.

Naz pointed to a small grassy patch near the camp, where a chocolate Swiss roll sat on a plate. One by one the flits lit a birthday candle and Impy led them all in a parade, carrying her candle like a torch and sticking it in the cake. The others followed until there was a line of thirteen candles.

And every single one of the flits was waving and jumping and whistling. Sami joined them, flapping her arms and punching the air, and then Impy flew up towards her and for the last time threw her arms around the ball of Edie's thumb.

Within two days they would all be gone, but Edie didn't feel scared any more. She felt for the tiny pebble in her pocket with I and E on it and focused as hard as she could on the row of cake candles burning like beacons to mark her thirteenth birthday.

Acknowledgements

A huge thank you . . .

To all at Piccadilly Press – Fliss for believing in Edie Winter, Maurice for staying with her through all the months of Covid and Ruth for editing her Parisian adventure with such patience and skill. To Emma, Molly and Antonia for promoting and banner waving and to Jenny and Holly for your eagle eyes. To Dom for your expertise with design and Joe Berger for your fabulous illustrations. Those covers are beauties!

To the London Transport Museum for your vintage Tube trains and for being a haven when I had two small 'London' boys. And to Hidden London for helping me discover the abandoned platforms and ghost stations of this city.

To Paul Cowan at the TfL Lost Property Office for showing me around, introducing me to the gorilla and allowing me to take dreadful liberties!

To independent bookshops everywhere that have stocked *Edie* – the true Davids in a world of not-so-friendly Goliaths. In particular to Olivia at Pickled Pepper in Crouch End and Sanchita at the Children's Bookshop in Muswell Hill.

To all the primary schools I've visited and especially to Rhodes Avenue and Alexandra Park School for being Edie's schools, and to Becky and Long Crendon's Year Six for being my very first critics.

To Bath Spa MAYWP 2018 – in particular to Julia Green, Steve Voake and Janine Amos and to the cabal of ex-students who continue to inspire, prop up and give everything a rigorous going-over – the Bradies, Lesley Parr, Jay Joseph and my current 'Steve Voake Thursday morning group'.

To 'Agent Helen' at Pickled Ink for taking on Edie Winter as a fledgling, for spotting a real-life Victor Rottier in St Germain and for just being an all-round superstar. I can't think of anyone else I'd rather be with!

To Frederique Michelle for tidying up my terrible O Level French.

To friends and family who have been incredibly supportive and especially to Ian, Jamie and Daniel for allowing me to endlessly disappear into my cupboard room above the front door and making me mugs of tea.

You are all safely stowed in my own flit box – lined with gold, of course!

And last, but not least, to the cities of London and Paris, to the mice at Highbury & Islington Underground where it all began and to YOU for deciding to read my story.

Make Your Own Flit Box

You can create your own perfect flit home in an old shoe box or crate. Using pieces of cardboard as walls, divide the space up into rooms and furnish them with recycled items you find at home or on the way to school. Try using Lego bricks for a table and corks for stools, maybe? Or a bottle top for a sink and a matchbox for a drawer? You can build the perfect flit box with a bit of imagination.

Meet the London Flits

Impy is a special flit as she has wings that are perfect for 'flitting about'. Her outfit is stitched together from brightly coloured sweet wrappers and she has an F7 forager badge. She's brave and loyal but likes telling everyone what to do.

Most likely to say: Never trust a magpin!

Nid has a tuft of hair that stands up like a pastry brush and he doesn't have wings. He likes to leap everywhere, climb up curtains and do star jumps. He's always getting into scrapes or juggling shiny beads, and he LOVES sugar.

Most likely to say: Yeee Haaaah! or Where's the Rice Krispies?

Jot and Speckle are twins and when Jot goes missing Speckle is distraught. He's shy and afraid of the dark.

Most likely to say: nothing (as he rarely speaks), but he's a brilliant artist and will draw a picture.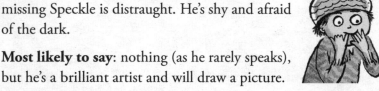

Pea is the youngest of the London flits and like all flits she was hatched out of a nut.

The London flits live in the Hillside Camp, which is built out of recycled rubbish they find in the Underground and set alongside the old tracks of a deserted station in Highgate.

Meet the Paris Flits

Enzo has a motorcycle and a helmet made out of a bottle top. He loves to drive at high speed around the pipework of the Lost Property Office with his scarf flying out behind him, and he bakes using the hot pipe in Fabien's tiny office as an oven.

Most likely to say: A croissant, anyone?

Mousette is Enzo's daughter and a very good cyclist. She wears a red beret, which she gives to Pea.

Most likely to say: Next stop the Paris Olympics!

Enzo and Mousette live in the Paris Lost Property Office in Fabien's tiny office but their family live on a deserted railway line known as La Petite Ceinture.

Albert is Enzo's brother and he has an apothecary for his potions and lotions in Jardin des Plantes, where the bees are his assistants.

Most likely to say: Tea tree oil might be good for that sting.

Leon and **Souris** live on a Metro platform at Bastille. They cycle around Paris via a network of gutters and drains.

Most likely to say: Vive la France!

Fun Facts about the London Underground

London Underground has 272 stations and twelve lines. It's one of the oldest and biggest underground networks in the world!

Arsenal is the only station named *after* a football club. It was originally called Gillespie Road.

It's estimated that half a million mice live in the tunnels and along the tracks.

You can see pictures of Sherlock Holmes on the platform walls at Baker Street.

Fun Facts about the Paris Metro

Arts et Métiers station is designed to look like a submarine.

There is a ghost station on the Paris Metro called Arsenal.

Every building in Paris is within 500 metres of a Metro station.

Concorde station has a giant word search puzzle on the wall.

Kate Wilkinson, author

Kate started out as a children's writer for BBC Radio creating audio stories for pre-school listeners that involved a lot of animals (and animal noises). She then became a radio producer for many years, recording everything from boiling spaghetti to a poet in a broom cupboard, and working primarily on arts programmes, literary features and readings such as Radio 4's *Book at Bedtime* and *Book of the Week*.

She completed the MA in Writing for Young People at Bath Spa University in 2018. Kate has two teenage boys and lives in North London with her partner, who is a news journalist.

What is your favourite station on the Underground?
Highbury and Islington

Have you ever lost anything on the Underground?
A Halloween cloak

Most likely to say:
Let's go by train!

Favourite French cake:
A chocolate eclair

Joe Berger, illustrator

Joe is a freelance illustrator who makes award-winning animations, and has also co-written and drawn a comic strip every week since 2003. He has written and illustrated many children's books and in 2010 was World Book Day Illustrator. He lives in Bristol.

What is your favourite station on the Underground?
Baker Street

Have you ever lost anything on the Underground?
A half-finished cryptic crossword

Most likely to say:
Boulanger's indulgence, we hear (5,6)

Favourite French cake:
A madeleine

Thank you for choosing a Piccadilly Press book.

If you would like to know more about our authors, our books or if you'd just like to know what we're up to, you can find us online.

www.piccadillypress.co.uk

And you can also find us on:

We hope to see you soon!